**"I had the imp**

**a week ago th**
**be work collea**
**more."**

His dark blue eyes were unfathomable, but she noticed a nerve flicker in his cheek. He sipped his wine before he said softly, "Is that what you want, Savannah?"

She was about to assure him that of course it was. Anything other than a strictly work-based relationship with Dimitris would be dangerous. But she was transfixed by his masculine beauty, and when he smiled, she felt more alive than she had in ten years. "I don't know," she admitted huskily.

The band had been playing smooth jazz tunes during dinner, but now the guests had finished eating and the tempo of the music increased as people stepped onto the dance floor.

Dimitris pushed back his chair and stood up. He offered his hand to Savannah. "Would you like to dance?"

**Chantelle Shaw** lives on the Kent coast and thinks up her stories while walking on the beach. She has been married for over thirty years and has six children. Her love affair with reading and writing Harlequin stories began as a teenager, and her first book was published in 2006. She likes strong-willed, slightly unusual characters. Chantelle also loves gardening, walking and wine.

**Books by Chantelle Shaw**

**Harlequin Presents**

*Proof of Their Forbidden Night*
*Her Wedding Night Negotiation*
*Housekeeper in the Headlines*
*The Italian's Bargain for His Bride*
*A Baby Scandal in Italy*

***Passionately Ever After...***

*Her Secret Royal Dilemma*

***Innocent Summer Brides***

*The Greek Wedding She Never Had*
*Nine Months to Tame the Tycoon*

Visit the Author Profile page
at Harlequin.com for more titles.

*Chantelle Shaw*

# PENNILESS CINDERELLA FOR THE GREEK

ISBN-13: 978-1-335-73945-2

Penniless Cinderella for the Greek



For questions and comments about the quality of this book, please contact us at CustomerService@Harlequin.com.

Harlequin Enterprises ULC
22 Adelaide St. West, 41st Floor
Toronto, Ontario M5H 4E3, Canada
www.Harlequin.com

**Printed in U.S.A.**

# PENNILESS CINDERELLA FOR THE GREEK

In memory of Julia, my wonderful mother-in-law.

# CHAPTER ONE

'WHAT CAN I get you, sir?' The barman dropped the cloth he had been pushing in a lacklustre fashion across the counter and stood straighter when he saw Dimitris. 'I hope you don't mind me mentioning that you look a lot like the celebrity chef Dimitris Kyriakou.'

'I have been told there is a resemblance,' Dimitris murmured drily. He had learned to live with the public recognition that fame had brought him, but this evening he was preoccupied and not inclined to chat to the barman. 'Give me a bottle of champagne and a couple of glasses, will you.'

'Certainly, sir. If you are a hotel guest I can arrange for the champagne to be delivered to your room.'

'I'll take it with me.' Dimitris smiled, but his eyes were hard. 'I'm planning a little surprise.' He masked his impatience while the barman placed two flutes on a tray, scooped ice into a bucket and took a bottle of champagne from the fridge.

'Are you celebrating a special event?' the young man asked chattily.

'Something like that.'

If his sister Eleni's suspicions about her fiancé were proved correct she had vowed to break off her engagement to Matt Collier. In Dimitris's opinion it would be a cause for celebration. He'd made some discreet enquiries and learned that Collier had a reputation for cheating on his previous girlfriends.

Eleni deserved to marry a man who would be a faithful and loving husband. Dimitris felt a pang when he thought of his parents' happy marriage before their lives were cut tragically short. He had agreed to help Eleni discover if Collier had a mistress because it was his duty to take care of his younger sister. After all, it was his fault that she had been orphaned when she was ten years old.

Dimitris was fourteen when their parents had been killed and Eleni had sustained life-changing injuries in a car accident. Amazingly he had escaped from the wreckage virtually unscathed. In the mirror behind the bar he could see the faint white line of the scar that ran down his cheek and was partially hidden by the dark stubble on his jaw.

Although his physical scar had faded he was still

haunted by his guilt that he had been responsible for the accident. In the past eighteen years Eleni had undergone numerous operations and for a long time she'd had to use a wheelchair or walking stick. Pioneering surgery meant that she would be able to walk down the aisle unaided on her wedding day, in three weeks' time, unless Dimitris found evidence that Eleni's slick advertising executive fiancé was a cheat.

*'Matt has been acting strangely lately. I know it was an awful thing to do, but while he was in another room I looked at his phone and discovered that he has been in regular contact with a woman he calls S,'* Eleni had sobbed. *'Matt told me he is going away at the weekend to play in a golf tournament, but his messages show that he has arranged to meet S at a hotel. I have to know the truth. You will help me, won't you, Dimitris?'*

Earlier, Dimitris had driven to the country house hotel a few miles out of London where Eleni's fiancé had arranged a secret assignation. Collier's car was in the car park and his phone messages to the mysterious *S* had included a room number. Dimitris had endured a mediocre dinner at the hotel, hoping to spot Collier and his companion. But they hadn't appeared in the dining room so he would have to implement Plan B.

He carried the tray with the champagne out of the bar and stepped into the lift.

* * *

'I'm going to take a quick shower, baby. Don't go anywhere!' Matt winked at Savannah and she forced a smile, but her face clouded over as she watched him saunter into the bathroom.

She couldn't go through with it. She could not sleep with Matt even though it was their third date, and everyone knew that the third date meant sex. It was one reason why she'd never got further than a second date in years. She'd disliked the pressure to rush into a sexual relationship. The truth was there had always been something missing when she'd dated other men and it hadn't been a difficult decision not to see them again. With Matt she'd felt a spark of attraction, and his open, friendly nature had allowed her to relax her usual wariness.

She reminded herself that they were both single, consenting adults. So what was the problem? The hotel suite's impersonal décor added to Savannah's sense that what they were about to do was sordid rather than romantic. Perhaps she would have felt better if Matt had suggested they could spend their first night together at his flat. He'd told her that he owned an apartment in Canary Wharf, but the decorators were in and the place was a mess.

Matt had arranged for them to have a private dinner in the suite. It was a thoughtful gesture, but Savannah had felt too uptight to eat much. Now she was relieved to be alone, although it was a temporary reprieve. She wandered around the room and raked her fingers through her hair—an unconscious habit when she felt tense.

*You are being idiotic*, she told her reflection in the mirror.

She tried to reassure herself that it was natural to feel apprehensive about having sex after a long gap. She could list her previous sexual experiences on the back of a postage stamp, but once she got started she would be fine.

Getting undressed would be a start. Her dress was a slinky wraparound style. She never usually wore red, but she'd chosen the seductive scarlet dress to boost her confidence. It hadn't worked and her fingers were unsteady as she untied the belt and the two sides of the dress fell open to reveal her black lace push-up bra, also new and bought in the hope that the sexy underwear would give her libido the wake-up call it needed.

Savannah cast her mind back to a couple of weeks ago when she'd met Matt Collier through her job as a food photographer. Her assignment had been to take pictures for an advertising campaign Matt had devised to promote a new tapas bar in Soho. She'd been drawn to his laid-back charm, and after the shoot it had seemed natural to stay on for a few drinks in the bar with him. In fact anything had been preferable to going home to face the dire financial situation her father had left behind.

Over dinner on their second date Matt had explained that his last relationship had ended a few months ago. Savannah had enjoyed his company and agreed to his suggestion to meet him at a hotel. Everything else in her life was going spectacularly wrong and she'd welcomed the distraction of a new relationship. Besides, she was twenty-eight and it was time she stopped hiding away from life.

'No one does old-fashioned courtship any more,' her agent and friend Bev had stated a few days ago when Savannah had confided that she was considering moving her relationship with Matt up a notch. If you like this guy, go for it. From the sound of it your ex-fiancé was a jerk, and you need to get over him.'

Years ago Savannah had ended her engagement to Hugo when she'd realised that she wasn't in love with him. Discovering that he had used her for his own nefarious reasons had been humiliating, but Hugo hadn't broken her heart. That honour went to the man who still invaded her dreams ten years after he had cruelly rejected her. Thinking about *him* had made her furious and she'd resolved to take Bev's advice and give Matt a chance.

But when Matt had ushered her into the suite and she'd seen the king-size bed she'd had an attack of doubts, or nerves, maybe both. It was too soon, and she wasn't ready to have a sexual relationship with someone she hardly knew. Maybe it was ridiculous to hope she would one day meet a man who made her heart pound and know she would willingly follow him to the ends of the earth. With a flash of clarity Savannah realised that she wasn't prepared to settle for less.

She heard the sound of the shower and briefly considered making her escape while Matt was in the bathroom. Her conscience pricked that it would be unfair to run out on him. He was a nice guy and deserved to know that the problem was her, not him.

A knock on the door of the suite gave her hope that the hotel was on fire, although presumably the fire alarm would be ringing. With any luck a sinkhole had opened up on the driveway and the guests were being advised to evacuate the hotel. Whatever the reason, the interruption was perfectly timed and would give her a chance to explain to Matt that she had changed her mind about them becoming lovers.

Savannah hurried to open the door and belatedly remembered that the front of her dress was undone.

The lift stopped at the fourth floor and Dimitris walked down the corridor and knocked on the door of Room 402. 'Room service.'

'Just a minute,' came a female voice from the other side of the door. 'Matt, did you order…?' Silence and then Dimitris heard her mutter, 'I suppose he can't hear me in the bathroom.'

The door opened, but the woman did not look at him while she fumbled to tie the belt of her scarlet dress. Dimitris wondered if she'd pulled her clothes on in a hurry. The front edges of her dress did not meet properly, affording him an enticing glimpse of the pale mounds of her breasts spilling over the top of her bra.

He took in her blonde hair that fell in messy waves to just above her shoulders, before raking his gaze over her slender figure and finally down to her long legs and scarlet stiletto-heeled shoes. The lady in red was a sexy little number. Her perfume was evocative, floral notes mixed with something deeper and more sensual that stirred a distant memory in Dimitris's mind, but it remained elusive.

'I'll put the champagne on the table, shall I?' He strode into the room without giving the woman time to reply. Rage burned in his gut. He was glad he'd persuaded Eleni to stay at home. His sister would be devastated when he confirmed that the man she loved did indeed have a mistress, but at least she had been spared the humiliation of coming face to face with the fragrant woman who, from her dishevelled hair and clothes, Dimitris assumed had moments ago been in bed with Eleni's fiancé.

A door that must lead to the en suite bathroom opened and Matt Collier emerged, wearing a bathrobe. His jaw sagged when he saw Dimitris. 'What the bloody hell are you doing here?'

Dimitris did not answer. He had realised why the woman's fragrance was familiar. It had haunted him for years. *She* had haunted him for years. She lifted her head and looked at him, and recognition flared in her hazel-green eyes as they widened with surprise.

*'Dimitris?'*

'Savannah O'Neal.' Shock ricocheted through him. He narrowed his gaze to hide his reaction as his brain, and more pertinently his body, acknowledged that the pretty teenager he'd dumped ten years ago had grown up to become a stunningly beautiful and very sexy woman. 'It's been a long time.'

Dimitris's effect on Savannah was as shattering as when she had been eighteen. Her heart was pounding and her mouth was dry. She had seen him on TV many times, hosting his hugely popular cooking programmes. His rock star looks and charismatic personality meant that he was regularly invited to be a guest on chat shows. But nothing had prepared Savannah for seeing him for real. His sex appeal was off the scale.

She had often imagined meeting Dimitris again and she'd planned on being cool and sophisticated, unlike the teenager who'd had a massive crush on him. The years fell away and she was the gauche girl on the cusp of womanhood who had day-dreamed that the handsome Greek god working in his family's restaurant would notice her. For eleven magical nights her fantasy had come true. But there had been no fairy tale happy ending, just a cold dose of reality that had forced her to grow up.

At twenty-two, Dimitris's swarthy good looks had made him seem exotic and gorgeous compared to the few boys of her age Savannah had known. She'd had a sheltered upbringing and been privately educated at an all-girls' school, and she had been ill-equipped to deal with Dimitris's potent masculinity. When he'd laughed, the wicked glint in his eyes had been irresistible. But there was no hint of laughter on his chiselled features, and he looked as though he'd been hewn from granite or cold, hard marble.

Now in his early thirties, he was even more devastatingly attractive than she remembered. The scar on his cheek had faded over time. It did not detract from his good looks, rather it gave him a piratical air that added to his intrigue. His square jaw was uncompromising and his cheekbones sharply angular. Eyes a fathomless dark blue were shaded by thick black lashes and his heavy brows met over a strong nose. But it was his mouth that held Savannah's attention. The full lips that promised heaven and had delivered, she remembered. His kiss was imprinted on her psyche.

She told herself that Dimitris, breaker of a thousand hearts besides her own, would have no memory of their first passionate encounter on a sultry summer's night a decade ago. But the gleam in his eyes made her wonder if his mind had revisited the pool house on the night of her eighteenth birthday party.

'It's not what it looks like.' Matt's voice jolted Savannah back to reality.

*Matt!*

She felt guilty at how easily she had forgotten him. It had been sweet of Matt to order champagne. Perhaps he had planned to celebrate after they'd made love for the first time, she thought guiltily, knowing that she still had to have an awkward conversation with him and tell him she'd changed her mind about sleeping with him.

But why on earth had the famous chef and TV personality Dimitris Kyriakou delivered champagne to the suite? Utterly bemused, Savannah wondered if Matt had arranged to surprise her with a visit from a celebrity—a bit like a stripper-gram, although Dimitris showed no sign of removing his clothes. A memory of his muscular naked body pressed against hers brought a flush of warmth to her face.

She looked at Matt and then back at the impressive Greek who dominated the room with his sheer presence. One of the few things Dimitris had told her about himself years ago was that his mother had been English, and he had inherited his six feet plus height from her side of the family.

At eighteen Savannah had been painfully naïve,

and unaware that men like Dimitris were a rarity. Now she knew better. Now she knew that every man faded into insignificance compared to Dimitris. Her confusion grew when she sensed angry vibes from him.

'What's going on?' Savannah asked Matt. But he did not look at her and spoke to Dimitris.

'I know it must seem suspicious that I'm at a hotel with a woman. But Savannah is a work colleague. She suggested meeting up to discuss a project and I had no idea that she'd booked a room with the intention of trying to persuade me to sleep with her.'

Savannah gasped. 'That's not true. You know full well that you asked me to spend the night with you.' When Matt avoided her gaze she appealed to Dimitris. 'Will you please tell me why you are here?'

Eyes the unfathomable blue of the deepest ocean swept over her and set every nerve-ending on her body alight. Dimitris's penetrating gaze gave Savannah the unsettling notion that he could see inside her head.

'Do you expect me to believe that you did not know your lover is engaged to be married?' he asked curtly.

'I expect you to believe it because it's the truth.' Her brief spurt of temper fizzled out as she tried to make sense of what Dimitris had said. 'There must be some kind of mistake. Matt isn't engaged to anyone. Are you… Matt?'

Matt's sheepish expression turned sullen and there was no need for him to say anything. Savannah released her breath slowly as her shock and disbelief morphed into anger and mortification. *Fool*, she castigated herself. Would she never learn that all men were liars? She included her father in that sweeping generalisation, and now she knew it was true of both men in the hotel suite.

She felt sick when she looked at Matt, with his hair damp from the shower he'd taken before he'd planned to have sex with her. She wondered how he would have reacted if they hadn't been interrupted and she'd admitted that she had changed her mind. Would he have tried to persuade her to sleep with him, knowing that he'd promised to marry someone else?

'Matt and I are not lovers,' she told Dimitris. He looked disbelieving and, following his gaze down, she discovered that the tie on her wrap dress had come loose again and the front was gaping open, revealing her bra and an embarrassing amount of cleavage. Blushing furiously, she jerked the edges of her dress together.

'It's the truth,' Matt confirmed quickly. 'I haven't slept with Savannah, and she means nothing to me. Meeting her tonight was a stupid mistake.'

'That's not the impression you gave me,' she said

sharply. Ironically, she'd had second thoughts about sleeping with Matt because she did not know him well enough. It was bad enough to be humiliated by Matt, but for it to happen in front of Dimitris made her wish she could wake up from what must surely be a nightmare.

Matt ignored her and spoke to Dimitris. 'Look, mate, I don't know how you found me, but there's no need to tell Eleni about tonight's little indiscretion, especially as nothing happened.'

'I am not your *mate*, Collier.' Dimitris's voice dripped with icy disdain. 'My sister read messages on your phone and discovered that you had lied about attending a golf tournament and planned to meet someone you referred to as S. I assume that person is Savannah.'

'Matt is engaged to *Eleni*?' At last Savannah understood the reason for Dimitris's barely suppressed fury. Years ago, he had been fiercely protective of his younger sister. 'I didn't know,' she whispered.

Odd little things made sense now. Matt had used her initial in texts, joking that typing her name took too long. She'd believed him when he'd said he was taking a break from social media because constantly being online sucked out your soul. Matt had gone to great lengths to deceive her, and she'd fallen for his lies.

Dimitris scowled at Matt. 'The wedding is off,

Collier. My sister will want nothing more to do with you after this.'

'Is that really Eleni's decision or have you decided for her, Kyriakou? I'll talk to her and convince her to give me another chance.' Matt's bravado slipped and he took a hasty step backwards when Dimitris's jaw hardened aggressively.

'Keep away from Eleni. I will do whatever it takes to protect her from scum like you,' Dimitris growled.

He flicked his cold gaze over Savannah. 'Does your lover know you are married?' His lip curled when she looked startled. 'Not long after I left London years ago, I heard that you had become engaged to a member of the English aristocracy. The wedding was expected to be the society event of the year.' He shook his head. 'You and Collier deserve each other.'

Before Savannah had a chance to gather her wits and defend herself, Dimitris strode out of the hotel suite. In his wake it felt as though an earthquake had struck, leaving her dazed and disorientated.

'You didn't mention anything about being married.' Matt had the cheek to sound affronted.

'I'm not,' she muttered. 'I was engaged, but I called the wedding off.'

'It looks like my engagement is off.' Matt seemed annoyed rather than upset. 'Kyriakou has never approved of me marrying his sister and Eleni will do what he says because he pays for everything, including the luxury flat in Canary Wharf that was meant to have been a wedding present for us. It's damned inconvenient. I've already given notice to leave my rented flat and I'll have to look for somewhere else to live.'

He moved closer to Savannah and ran his finger down her cheek. 'Perhaps I could come and live with you at your big house near Hampstead Heath. What do you say we open the champagne and drink to new beginnings, baby?'

She jerked away from him in disgust. 'You've got a nerve. I hope I never see you again. Anyway, it's my mother's house.'

But in fact Pond House did not belong to her mother, Savannah thought bleakly. It had been yet another shock to discover that the title deed of the house only bore her father's name, meaning that the property was an asset of Richard O'Neal's. His creditors were demanding that the house must be sold to pay his debts.

Savannah remembered how Matt had been impressed with the house where she had grown up, and had returned to live after her mum had become ill, when he'd dropped her home after their second date. He had remarked that properties in the area were worth a fortune. Pond House, with its private swimming pool, tennis court and extensive grounds, had recently been valued at several million pounds. The sale of the house should raise enough money to clear her father's debts, but Savannah knew it would break her mother's heart to leave the home she loved.

'Get lost, Matt.' She did not know who she loathed most—Matt for being a creep, or herself for having been so gullible. 'Why did you start dating me when you were planning to marry someone else?'

He shrugged. 'It was obvious when we had drinks after the photoshoot that you were available and a bit desperate. I thought I'd covered my tracks and Eleni wouldn't find out. Most blokes will seize an opportunity if it comes their way,' he said sulkily. 'Kyriakou can't take the moral high ground. He's a notorious womaniser and lurid details about his personal life regularly appear in the tabloids.'

Savannah had seen photos in the newspapers of Dimitris with a seemingly never-ending supply of beautiful women. Since his meteoric rise to fame as a celebrity chef who had amassed a multi-million-pound fortune from his bestselling cookery books, numerous TV appearances and a chain of hugely successful Greek restaurants, Dimitris was regarded as a highly eligible bachelor. Unfortunately for his legions of female fans, he was determined to maintain his single status and was on record saying that he had no desire to marry and settle down.

He'd said the same thing ten years ago when Savannah had laid her heart on the line and told him that she loved him. Remembering how naïve she had been made her cringe. She was dismayed that Dimitris still had a seismic effect on her. Her body was tingling all over, and he made her feel more alive and aware of her femininity than any other man ever had.

'What's the story between you and Kyriakou?' Matt sounded petulant. 'Why did he recognise you?'

'I...knew him a long time ago.' Her short affair with Dimitris had been passionate and intense, and she'd been obsessed with him, but she had not really known him. Savannah wondered if any woman had managed to break through the steel barrier around his emotions.

She was angry that he hadn't given her a chance to explain how she had been duped by Matt. She did not care about Dimitris's opinion of her, she assured herself. But she had been friends with Eleni, and she wanted to set the record straight about her involvement with Matt Collier.

'Don't try to contact me again,' she told Matt as she gathered up her bag and the shreds of her dignity and hurried out of the suite. Up ahead she saw Dimitris was about to step into the lift.

*'Wait!'* Savannah tore along the corridor. The doors were sliding closed, and she shoved her hand between them so that they automatically opened

again. Time juddered to a standstill as she stared into the lift at Dimitris. Her nemesis.

His black hair was cut shorter than Savannah remembered, but it still had a tendency to curl. He was a work of art, beyond merely handsome. Anger emanated from his whipcord body. 'I don't have time for this,' he grated. 'I must go to my sister.'

Savannah's eyes were drawn to the glint of the gold watch on his wrist that contrasted with his olive-toned skin. His sleeves were rolled up to the elbows and his forearms were covered with black hairs. Wearing black trousers and a shirt, and with a scowl on his face, he was a dark avenging angel, determined to protect his sister from being hurt by *her*, Savannah thought bleakly. She had been an unwitting accomplice in Matt's cheating. It did not make her feel better knowing that they hadn't actually had sex.

'I didn't sleep with Matt,' she repeated. There was no softening of Dimitris's hard features. Savannah bit her lip. 'Please don't tell Eleni that you found me with her fiancé. She and I were friends before we lost touch, and I would never do anything to hurt her.'

Dimitris's silence was damning, but with a jolt Savannah recognised a gleam of awareness in his eyes. Ten years ago their chemistry had been white-hot. She moved her hand up to the front of her dress to check it was still fastened and the lift doors instantly closed. Cursing, she jabbed her finger on the button to open the doors again, but the indicator arrow showed that the lift had started to descend.

She sagged against the wall, breathing hard as if she'd run a marathon. It was crazy how hurt she felt by Dimitris's refusal to listen to her. He had accepted at face value finding her with his sister's fiancé and had judged her unfairly. Even worse, seeing Dimitris again had forced Savannah to face the truth that she had tried to deny to herself since she was eighteen. She had never got over him and she compared all other men to him.

# CHAPTER TWO

'IS SHE PRETTY?'

Dimitris raised an eyebrow. 'Who?' He was aware that he was playing for time before he answered his sister, but he wanted to be sure his emotions were under control. He did not like surprises like the one he'd had earlier tonight.

'Matt's other woman, of course.' Eleni wiped away her tears. She'd been crying ever since Dimitris had returned to his house in Richmond upon Thames, where his sister had come to stay while she prepared for her wedding, and gently broken the news that he'd found Collier at the hotel with a woman who was evidently his mistress.

'I did not take much notice of her.' Dimitris hated deceit, but he made no apology for the lie. *Theós!* He wasn't going to admit to Eleni or himself that when he'd recognised Savannah his heart had crashed against his ribs with the force of a runaway juggernaut. He saw no point in revealing to his sister that her now ex-fiancé's mistress was none other than Eleni's old schoolfriend.

It was not the first time Dimitris had seen Savannah since he'd broken off their relationship, but photographs could not fully capture her intriguing mix of innocence and sensuality. Her image had graced billboards in major cities around the world when she had been 'the face' of a well-known cosmetics company and she'd also modelled for a designer brand of eyewear.

Savannah possessed exquisite facial features and her hazel-green eyes were mesmerising. Dimitris knew that their stunning colour had not been enhanced by the latest photographic technology. Her eyes were the first thing he had noticed about her when she'd been a teenager and had applied for a summer waitressing job in his grandfather's restaurant.

'Savannah is not like most of the other rich girls at school,' Eleni had assured him when he'd been doubtful that the daughter of a wealthy businessman would be willing to work long hours for low wages. Hestia's Authentic Greek restaurant, situated at the rough end of the high street in a north London borough, had been struggling to attract customers since several fast food places had opened up nearby.

'She has never made me feel embarrassed about being the only scholarship pupil at Brampton Girls Academy, or that I use a wheelchair,' Eleni had said.

'Savannah is my friend. Please give her a chance, Dimitris. I'm sure you won't be disappointed with her.'

Dimitris swore silently as he was bombarded by memories of Savannah's shy smile, her slender figure and pert curves, and the way she'd blushed when he had caught her watching him. At twenty-two he had been used to receiving attention from women, and he'd dated widely but never exclusively. He had told himself that Savannah was too young, and her air of vulnerability made her off-limits. He could not offer her a meaningful relationship that he sensed she hoped for.

It was a pity he hadn't listened to the warning voice inside his head, he brooded. Their affair had been short-lived, and Dimitris had moved away. But he'd never quite forgotten the heady passion that had burned out of control between them. Ten years was a long time and people changed. He certainly had, and he should not be surprised that the half-undressed siren he'd discovered in a hotel room with the man Eleni had hoped to marry was different to the sweet girl he'd known a decade ago, who had affected him more deeply than he cared to admit.

A couple of months after he'd broken up with Savannah, he'd been working as a chef at a hotel in Rhodes and had flicked through an English newspaper. He'd been shocked to read about her engagement to the son of an earl or a duke—Dimitris could not recall the exact details. He had felt gutted that she'd made plans to marry another man so soon after she had declared her love for him. But he'd reminded himself that he did not deserve to be loved after he had destroyed the two people who had loved him most.

He guessed that Savannah's father had approved of her marrying into the aristocracy. Thinking of Richard O'Neal reminded Dimitris of the deal he had been forced to make with Savannah's father, and the secret that he'd kept from her.

He forced his mind from the distant past and frowned as he replayed the scene in the hotel suite. Savannah had denied knowing that Matt Collier was engaged, and she had seemed shocked. But they lived in an age when most people's personal details were plastered over social media. She *must* have known that Collier had promised to marry Eleni, Dimitris thought grimly.

'I bet Matt's girlfriend doesn't walk with a limp.' Eleni's face crumpled. 'I know you had doubts about Matt. I wish I had listened to you. I'll have to call the caterers and the florist and all the guests to tell them the wedding is cancelled. I was due to have a final fitting of my dress, but I won't get to wear it now.'

'Hush, *paidí mou.*' Dimitris put his hand on his sister's shoulders that were shaking with the force of her sobs. He had spent his whole adult life taking care of Eleni, but at this moment he felt helpless. Her distress fuelled his anger with Matt Collier and Savannah for hurting her. 'I will deal with everything and cancel the wedding arrangements. Go to bed and try to sleep.'

Guilt, his ever-present demon, slid a knife-blade between his ribs as he watched Eleni walk stiffly across the room. It was a miracle she was able to walk at all. For the past decade Dimitris had regularly worked eighteen-hour days, he'd seized every opportunity that had come his way and he was the first to admit that he'd had some lucky breaks. He had poured his passion into cooking and earned a fortune, and he was driven by a desire to try to recompense his sister for ruining her life.

He would never forgive himself for causing the accident that had destroyed his happy family. If he hadn't distracted his mother, so that she had taken her eyes off the road, their car would not have swerved into the path of an oncoming lorry.

After all this time Dimitris still suffered flashbacks. He had been a troubled teenager, torn between his Greek and English cultures, and he'd felt he did not belong anywhere. He'd been drawn into a gang of older boys who had used and sold drugs on the streets. With hindsight Dimitris realised that his parents had been trying to protect him when they'd refused to let him stay out late, but at fourteen he'd resented their rules and curfews.

On that fateful day his parents had been taking Eleni to her dance class, and he should have ridden his bike to football training, but he'd overslept, and his mum had agreed to give him a lift. The argument had started in the car.

*'Would you mind helping in the restaurant this evening, Dimitris? One of the waitresses is ill.'*

*'Oh, Mum. It's Saturday night, and everyone's meeting at Jack's house.'*

*'Well, you can go out with your friends, but I want you home by eleven. Dad will collect you so that you don't have to walk back on your own.'*

*'Stop treating me like a kid. No one else's parents make a fuss. Can I at least stay out until midnight?'*

*'It's too late. And you've got homework to finish tomorrow. Eleni said she saw you playing games on your computer instead of getting on with your history project.'*

*'Thanks for snitching, Eleni. Stay out of my room in future.'*

Eleni had started to cry. Both parents had turned their heads to look at Dimitris in the back of the car.

*'Don't be mean to your sister,'* his mother had told him. Her voice had softened. *'Your family are concerned about you because we love you.'*

Dimitris had seen the lorry the split-second before the crash. *'Mum—look out!'*

His jaw clenched as he fought to block out his

agonising memories. He focused on Eleni when she paused in the doorway. 'I want to go back to Greece,' she said in a choked voice. 'At least I hadn't relocated my business to London. What will happen to the flat in Canary Wharf?'

'I'll sell it or rent it out.' Dimitris sighed. 'I know it's hard to believe now, but one day you will meet the right person who will make you happy.'

Eleni sniffed. 'You haven't.'

'Ah, but I don't want to fall in love.'

'I'm not sure we can control these things. Love just happens and it creeps up when you are least expecting it.'

'Not to me it doesn't,' Dimitris said firmly. He had decided when he was fourteen and racked with grief and guilt that he must spend the rest of his life alone. He did not deserve the things that most people took for granted, such as falling in love and having a family of his own.

'Will you come to Rhodes with me?' Eleni pleaded. 'I can't face telling *Γιαγιά* that my wedding is cancelled.'

Their grandmother Hestia was a formidable matriarch even at nearly ninety. Dimitris shook his head regretfully. 'I must stay in London to take part in the photoshoot for Philpot's. As soon as I am free I'll join you at the villa.'

After Eleni had gone upstairs, Dimitris checked his messages on his phone. He had agreed to become the brand ambassador for Philpot's, the UK's biggest supermarket chain, in return for their support of his charity Food for All, which was involved in a number of projects to encourage young people to learn to cook instead of relying on fast food.

There was an email from Philpot's PR executive regarding the photography session the next day, when Dimitris would cook the dishes he had created for the supermarket's Healthy Meals campaign. The recipes and accompanying photographs of the food would be published in the autumn edition of Philpot's magazine. He had left all the arrangements to their PR team while he'd been concerned about his sister, and this was the first time he'd looked at the details of the shoot.

Philpot's had commissioned an up-and-coming food photographer. Dimitris cursed as the name jumped out at him. Savannah O'Neal. *Seriously?* What were the chances that there were two women with the same fairly unusual name? Fate had a warped sense of humour, he thought grimly.

Savannah woke to blinding sunshine streaming through the half-open curtains. She squinted at the clock on the bedside cabinet and groaned when she realised that she must have switched off the alarm and fallen back to sleep. It was eight a.m., and she had a full-on day at work in front of her. She'd packed her camera gear last night, but there was an element of secrecy around the shoot, and she hadn't been told yet where it would take place. Hopefully the location wasn't miles away.

As she scrambled out of bed her phone rang. Guessing it was her agent with details of the photo-shoot, she flung her hand out to pick up her phone and knocked over a glass of water. *'Dammit.'*

'Bad news, I'm afraid,' Beverly Wright, owner of Wright's Photographic Agency and known to everyone as Bev, greeted Savannah.

'I've had my quota of bad news for this century.' What else could go wrong? Savannah ran her mind over the events of the past year, when her father had been arrested and convicted of corruption. Before he could begin his lengthy prison sentence he had died from a heart attack. Savannah was still trying to come to terms with his death, and the shocking revelations in court that her apparently respectable and successful businessman father had committed fraud on a breathtaking scale.

Dating Matt Collier had allowed her to temporarily forget the stress of dealing with her father's financial affairs and her worries about her mum. But Matt had shown himself to be as unreliable as every other man Savannah had known.

As for Dimitris, she had been stunned when he'd appeared in the hotel suite, and horrified by her body's instant response to him. Forget Sleeping Beauty who had been woken by the handsome prince's kiss. All it had taken was one searing look from Dimitris to rekindle her libido. Memories of the shockingly erotic dream she'd had about him last night evoked a flood of warmth between her thighs.

'What news?' she croaked into her phone.

'Philpot's have cancelled.'

'But the shoot was meant to be today. Are they going to reschedule?' Savannah sank down onto the bed. 'Let me know the new date and I'll make sure I'm available.'

Her work diary was not brimming with assignments. When she'd started out as a freelance photographer she'd realised it would take time to build her reputation, and she'd been lucky enough to have the back-up of her savings from her brief modelling career. But since her father's arrest, and after Richard O'Neal's assets had been frozen, most of her money had gone on household bills; her mother did not have money to pay for the upkeep of Pond House.

'The photoshoot is to go ahead today, but Philpot's have asked for a different photographer,' Bev told her. 'I'm sorry, Savannah. Tara Brown, head of brand communication, called me late last night and said that the request for you to be replaced came from the very top. As you know, the shoot is for the campaign Philpot's are planning for the autumn, when they will reveal that their new brand ambassador is the hot Greek chef Dimitris Kyriakou.'

Savannah made a muffled sound somewhere between a sob and hysterical laughter, but Bev did not seem to hear her.

'Actually I shouldn't have let that slip. Philpot's want to keep his identity under wraps until the launch, but I know I can trust you to keep it to yourself. Kyriakou prefers to work in his own kitchen studio and the photoshoot will be at River Retreat in Richmond, where his recent cooking series was filmed. I have no idea why he asked for a change of photographer. Perhaps he wasn't keen on your portfolio, although Philpot's loved your work. I tried calling you last night to let you know, but you didn't answer your phone.'

'I must have been in the bath.' After Savannah had left Matt at the hotel and driven home, she'd switched off her phone before taking a long soak, hoping it would help her relax after what was up there as one of the worst evenings of her life. Today wasn't proving to be much better.

'Luckily Philpot's are willing to use another photographer from my agency.' Bev was a businesswoman first and foremost. 'Jason Bloomfield will take your place. I've sent your portfolio to the editor of a lifestyle magazine who is planning an article about artisan bread.' Her tone softened. 'I know you must be disappointed about the Philpot's assignment, but these things happen.'

After the call from Bev, Savannah resisted the childish urge to hurl her phone across the room. The photoshoot for Philpot's would have raised her profile as a food photographer. Losing the assignment was a disaster both professionally and for her bank balance that was currently in the red.

She wasn't just disappointed; she was furious with Dimitris for being so petty and demanding that she was replaced by a different photographer. She had done nothing wrong. Matt Collier had deceived her as much as Eleni. Even so, she felt guilty that she had unwittingly been partly responsible for ruining her old schoolfriend's wedding plans. Her heart ached as she imagined how distraught Eleni must be feeling.

At eighteen Savannah had been devastated when Dimitris had bluntly told her that he was not in love with her. He had broken her heart, and now he had the power to potentially damage her career—unless she could convince him that she was not his sister's fiancé's mistress. Last night, when he had found her with Matt in the hotel room, Dimitris had been understandably angry and protective of his sister. But perhaps by now his temper had cooled and he would allow her to explain.

She did not have much time, Savannah realised. The photoshoot was scheduled to start at ten o'clock, but the team of assistants, food stylists and technicians would arrive earlier. If she left immediately and the London traffic wasn't too bad she could be in Richmond in just over half an hour. She prayed that her car would start. It was old and had been playing up recently, but the precarious state of her finances meant she couldn't afford to buy a newer model or take the car to a garage for it to be serviced.

Without wasting any more time, Savannah pulled on her usual work uniform of black trousers and tee shirt, scooped her hair into a ponytail and waved a mascara wand over her eyelashes before she ran downstairs. She met Cathy, her mother's live-in carer, outside the drawing room that had been turned into Evelyn's bedroom since her mobility had become affected by multiple sclerosis.

'Is Mum awake? How did she sleep?'

Cathy nodded. 'She had a fairly good night. I'm going to make Evelyn a cup of tea. Would you like one?' It had become a morning ritual for Savannah to spend time with her mum before she went to work.

'I can't hang about this morning. I've got to dash.' Savannah stepped into the room and felt a surge of love and concern when she noted how frail her mum looked, propped against the pillows.

The traumas of the past few years had taken a toll on Evelyn's health and mental wellbeing and her MS symptoms had worsened. It was hardly surprising after she'd had to cope with her husband's arrest and trial, his shocking death, and the dramatic change to her financial circumstances. Savannah tried to keep the truth of how broke they were from her mum. She had prioritised paying Cathy's wages because Evelyn needed the help of a carer as her health deteriorated, but finding the money was a struggle.

She walked over to the bed and leaned down to kiss her mother's cheek. 'I've got an early start this morning, Mum.'

'Oh, yes, today is the photoshoot for Philpot's, isn't it? Do you know which celebrity chef you'll be working with?'

Savannah tried to sound casual. 'I'm not supposed to tell a soul. He's Dimitris Kyriakou.'

Evelyn wasn't fooled. 'Be careful, darling. He upset you badly when you were younger.'

'I admit I fancied him like crazy for a while. I doubt he'll remember me, and all I'm going to do is take pictures of his food.' Except that she wasn't, Savannah thought after she'd left her mum. The assignment had been given to another photographer, but if she could persuade Dimitris to look at her portfolio and endorse her work, Philpot's might employ her for their future campaigns.

Richmond upon Thames was renowned for being an affluent area of south-west London, where millionaires were drawn to the leafy suburb close to the capital. Recently, an interview with Dimitris and photographs of him at his London home had been published in the magazine supplement of a Sunday newspaper. Savannah had bought the paper because it featured an article about photography that she'd wanted to read, or so she'd told herself. Admittedly she had been curious about Dimitris, and it was lucky she had studied the pictures in the magazine so intently because when she arrived in Richmond and drove past exclusive properties that backed onto the river she recognised his house, River Retreat.

She parked her car in the road and, out of habit, took her camera bag with her. Savannah hadn't made a plan of what she would do next. There was a good chance that Dimitris would refuse to speak to her. The gates were unlocked. Tension made her heart thud as she walked up the driveway to the front door and rang the bell.

A woman who seemed to be the housekeeper opened the door and glanced at her camera bag. 'You're here for the photoshoot,' she said before Savannah could introduce herself. 'Mr Kyriakou's kitchen studio is in the garden. Follow the path round to the back of the house and the studio is at the bottom of the lawn, next to the river.'

So far so easy. Savannah let out a soft sigh as she came round the corner of the house and took in the view of the sweeping green lawn bordered by flower beds filled with colourful blooms. Everywhere was immaculate and even the most determined weed would not dare poke through a gap in the patio stones, due no doubt to the vigilance of a full-time gardener.

She thought of the garden at Pond House that had been her mother's pride and joy. Evelyn no longer had the energy for gardening and the shrubs had gone wild. Savannah hoped that when the house was sold and she'd paid her father's creditors, there would be enough money left to buy an adapted bungalow for Evelyn and her carer to live in. But she would still need to earn a good income so that she could provide for her mum.

If word got around that the famous chef Dimitris Kyriakou had refused to work with her, people would think he was unimpressed with her photography, and it could have serious implications for her career. It was ironic that she and Dimitris had experienced a dramatic reversal of fortunes, Savannah thought. She had been brought up accustomed to wealth and privilege and it was deeply shocking to discover that her father had made his money from corrupt business dealings.

Her mother had been completely unaware of her husband's criminal activities. Growing up, Savannah's relationship with her father had been difficult and she'd tried to live up to his impossibly high standards. Since his trial, when she'd learned the truth about him, she'd felt as though the very fabric of her life and identity had been ripped away.

When she'd first met Dimitris he had lived in a small flat above his family's restaurant with his grandparents and sister. Several years earlier, their parents had been killed in a car accident and Eleni had sustained serious injuries that meant she used a wheelchair. Eleni had said she did not remember anything of the accident. Savannah had asked Dimitris what had happened, but he'd refused to talk about the tragedy. He hadn't told her anything really about himself. His emotions had been a closed book, but she was so wrapped up in being in love with him she had convinced herself that he felt the same way about her.

A trip down memory lane was not helpful right now, Savannah told herself as she continued along the path towards the timber and glass building that she recognised from Dimitris's cooking shows as his kitchen studio. His biography online stated that he had first been taught to cook by his grandfather, a Greek immigrant who had settled in London and opened a restaurant that he'd named Hestia's after his wife.

Dimitris had gone to college and trained as a professional chef. He'd helped run the restaurant before he and his grandparents and sister had suddenly moved to Greece. In Rhodes he had been sous chef at a top hotel. Later he'd moved to Paris, where he had become the chef de cuisine at one of the city's most prestigious restaurants. He had taken part in a cooking competition to find the best chef in Europe. The final had been broadcast live on television in England, and Dimitris had won and caught the attention of a TV producer who had given him his own televised cooking series.

*An Adonis in the Kitchen* had launched Dimitris's career as a celebrity chef and sex symbol in Europe and America, where he was hugely popular. Other series had followed. *Cooking with the Greek*, *Dinner with Dimitris* and *A Date with Dimitris* showcased his enthusiasm for cooking while his disarming personality and blatant sex appeal had earned him the nickname the Hot Chef.

Dimitris's impressive London house was proof that his single-minded determination to succeed had paid dividends. Savannah stood and watched the stately River Thames, so wide and blue and sparkling in the sunshine of what promised to be another glorious summer's day. A sleek motor cruiser moored next to the private jetty added to the sense of unobtrusive luxury.

'What are you doing trespassing on my property, Savannah?'

The gravelly voice from behind her made Savannah's heart lurch. She turned slowly, trying to prepare herself for the impact of seeing Dimitris again. But it was hopeless, and her breath rushed from her lungs as she met his sapphirine gaze.

# CHAPTER THREE

THE STUDIO'S BI-FOLD doors were open, and Savannah wondered how long Dimitris had been standing there. He looked divine in faded jeans that hugged his lean hips and a white jersey top clinging to the defined ridges of his muscular torso.

'You shouldn't be here,' he said curtly. 'Someone at Philpot's was supposed to tell the agency to send a different photographer.'

'I wanted to talk to you…' She found herself talking to Dimitris's back when he swung round and strode across the studio.

Savannah followed him inside. The kitchen studio was a large, light-filled space with a glass roof and furnished with pale wood units against the bare brick walls. An island with a hob stood in the middle of the room and behind it were professional ovens, sinks and more worktops.

The heavenly smell of freshly baked bread filled the air. Her stomach grumbled when she saw rolls cooling on a rack. She hadn't had time for breakfast and had barely eaten anything when she'd been at the hotel with Matt. Her cheeks burned at the memory of the humiliating events of the previous evening.

'I'll call Philpot's to find out why my instructions were not followed.'

If he spoke to Tara Brown the PR manager would contact Bev to ask if a replacement photographer had been assigned to the shoot. Savannah knew that her visit to Dimitris's home would be highly embarrassing for her agent. Bev should not have broken the client's confidentiality and revealed that Dimitris was Philpot's new brand ambassador.

'I'm not here for the photoshoot. If you would let me explain…'

'I have nothing to say to you.'

His dismissive tone was the last straw. Anger rolled in a red mist through her. The hunger pangs in her stomach were vying with the ache in her heart. Dimitris's riverside studio in the grounds of his beautiful house emphasised how different their lives had become. Savannah did not resent his success, but she was scared of what losing Pond House would do to her mum's physical and emotional health.

Her job as a photographer gave her a vital source of income and some much-needed personal pride, but with one phone call Dimitris could ruin everything she cared about. His phone was on the counter. As he stretched his hand towards it Savannah shot past him and grabbed the phone.

'I don't want you to *say* anything,' she told him fiercely. 'I want you to *listen*.'

His eyes darkened to the blue-black of obsidian as he glowered down at her from his superior height. She inhaled the spicy scent of his aftershave, and something visceral twisted in her stomach that in turn made her furious for being so weak. She could not allow him to affect her the way he had when she'd been an impressionable teenager.

'I am not Matt Collier's mistress. I went on a couple of dates with him after he'd told me he was single. At the risk of repeating myself, I had no idea he was Eleni's fiancé. I don't know why I'm surprised that Matt lied,' Savannah said bitterly. 'I've never met a man yet who was capable of telling the truth.'

Dimitris's scowl deepened, but Savannah refused to be cowed. She had been lied to all her life—by her father, her ex-fiancé Hugo, Matt Collier, who had dented her pride but not her heart, she acknowledged honestly, and Dimitris, who she'd put on a pedestal years ago.

'It's none of your business, but I have never been married.'

Dimitris's expression was inscrutable. Savannah remembered that even when he'd been younger he had kept a tight control over his emotions. It had made his fierce passion all the more exciting, knowing she had broken through his barricades. 'I never lied to you,' he said brusquely.

She rolled her eyes. 'Oh, please. When you ended our relationship you said it was so that you could concentrate on your career. But I know my father gave you money to dump me. He told me that he had been suspicious of your motives and as a test he offered you two hundred and fifty thousand pounds to break up with me.'

Savannah's satisfaction that she'd finally had a chance to confront Dimitris about what he had done was mixed with gut-wrenching disappointment when a startled look flickered on his handsome features. His guilty expression confirmed what her father had told her. Ten years ago Dimitris had chosen money over her.

'I'm not sure what I found more insulting. The fact that you used me for sex, or that you accepted a bribe to dump me,' she said sarcastically. 'Either way, you are no better than Matt Collier. I'm not defending him,' she insisted when Dimitris's jaw hardened. 'Matt lied to Eleni and to me. But you acted no better when you deceived me.'

'I never used you for sex. But, in hindsight, I realise I should not have got involved with you.' He frowned. 'You were young and ridiculously innocent, and not only because you were a virgin. You wanted a fairy tale that I couldn't give you.'

She felt her cheeks burn. 'When we made love it was amazing for both of us. You let me think we had a future.'

He shook his head. 'You wove a fantasy of happy ever after. But you were about to go to university and had your whole future in front of you. I had a failing restaurant to manage, and elderly grandparents and a disabled sister to take care of. I had nothing to offer you.' Dimitris hesitated. 'Did your father tell you anything else?'

'What do you mean?' Savannah grimaced as she thought of everything her father *hadn't* told her about his business empire that had been built on corruption and lies.

On the surface her family had appeared to be perfect, with her a spoiled only child whose father doted on her. But from a young age she had been aware that Richard O'Neal did not love her, despite all her attempts to please him and win his approval. She had wondered, and still did, if there was something wrong with her for her own father not to have cared about her. Dimitris's rejection had reinforced the feeling that she was somehow unlovable.

At his trial her father had been exposed as a serial fraudster. Savannah was angry that she had allowed him to dominate her life while she'd striven to be the perfect daughter. Now she was furious that another powerful man could influence her life, her career and, most importantly, her income that she badly needed so that she could look after her mum.

The tense silence in the studio shattered when Dimitris's phone rang. His expression was sardonic as he held out his hand for her to return his phone. She noticed the name Tara Brown on the screen. It had been a waste of time throwing herself on Dimitris's mercy, Savannah thought bitterly.

On the counter was a mixing bowl containing a thick, pale liquid that looked like pancake batter. Frustration bubbled up inside her, and without pausing to consider the consequences she dropped Dimitris's phone into the batter.

He swore. 'Why the hell did you do that?'

'I didn't want you to complain about me to Tara Brown,' Savannah muttered. 'I really needed the Philpot's assignment.' She had burned her bridges now. The awfulness of what she had done was sinking in faster than Dimitris's phone had sunk to the bottom of the bowl of gloop.

His jaw hardened and she sensed that he was containing his anger with an effort. His steely self-control made Savannah feel even more idiotic. She wanted to provoke a reaction from him, and if that reaction was blazing fury that matched her own, so much the better.

She gasped as Dimitris's arm shot out with the deadly speed of a cobra, and he captured her hand in his firm grip. A sensation like an electrical current shot from her fingertips, all the way up her arm and spread through her body. She prayed he did not notice that her nipples had hardened and were jutting through her tee shirt.

He pushed her hand down into the bowl of batter mixture. She curled her fingers around his phone and when she lifted it out of the bowl, blobs of batter dripped onto the worktop.

'I will expect you to reimburse me for the cost of a new phone.'

That was a joke. His phone was an exclusive and very expensive brand, but her savings were almost depleted and she could not afford to pay for a replacement device. The most sensible thing to do would be to apologise profusely to Dimitris and claim temporary insanity if he decided to prosecute her for wilfully damaging his property. But the word sorry stuck in Savannah's throat.

Anger burned inside her. She had been her father's dutiful daughter and Dimitris's devoted lover, but both men had betrayed her and rejected her love. All her life she had suppressed her emotions, mindful that her father would disapprove of any bad behaviour. She had wanted his approval, his *love*, so badly, just as she had longed for Dimitris to love her years ago. Now she discovered that rebelliousness was empowering.

Saying nothing, she lifted her hand and wiped the phone down the front of Dimitris's shirt, smearing him with batter mixture. His eyes narrowed and gleamed dangerously, but Savannah was past caring. Her reputation for professionalism was in tatters and things couldn't get any worse. She wiped his phone over his shirt a second time. It felt so good to be bad.

There was a warning glint in Dimitris's dark blue gaze as he snatched the phone out of her fingers and dropped it onto the counter. Savannah braced herself for his anger, but he merely raised his brows and his mouth curved into a mocking smile.

'If you are so desperate for me to take my shirt off, you only had to ask,' he drawled.

Savannah stopped breathing when he grasped the hem of his top and lifted it slowly over his head to reveal his bare bronzed chest, overlaid with black body hairs that arrowed down his taut abdomen and disappeared beneath the waistband of his jeans. She could not recall if she had moved or he had, but they were standing so close that she breathed in the spicy scent of his aftershave.

'I…' She wanted to deny his suggestion that she'd hoped he would remove his shirt, but her tongue had cleaved to the roof of her mouth, and all she could do was stare at him and drink in his male beauty with eyes that felt like they were stretched too wide. It was like staring at the sun, and she was dazzled by him. If she lowered her lashes she knew his image would be imprinted on her retinas.

He had haunted her dreams for a decade, but this was no fantasy. Dimitris was real. Compelled by a need she did not fully understand to evoke a response from him, she laid her hand on his naked chest and felt the erratic thud of his heart mimic her own frantic heartbeat.

'You should not have come here, Savannah,' he said harshly as he clamped his hand over hers where it lay on his chest and dragged it down. Embarrassed that she had touched him, she was about to move away. But with a curse he wrapped his arm around her waist and hauled her towards him so that her breasts were crushed against the hard wall of his ribcage. She lifted her stunned gaze and found his face so close to hers that she could have counted his eyelashes if her attention hadn't been fixated on his mouth.

Ten years ago their chemistry had sizzled if they had so much as looked at each other, but Savannah's inexperience meant she had not understood her feminine power. Last night, and again now, she recognised the hungry gleam of desire in Dimitris's eyes and her heart thudded as she waited in breathless anticipation for him to kiss her.

He lowered his head until his lips almost met hers. His warm breath whispered across her skin, and she could not repress a shiver of longing as she inhaled the subtle scent of sweat and desire on his skin. But then, shockingly, he reared back and set her away from him, dropping his arm down to his side abruptly, so that she swayed on her feet.

*'Theós!'* he bit out savagely. His breathing was laboured, and she sensed that his control was as balanced on a knife-edge as hers was.

His rejection lacerated her fragile emotions, and her brain urged her to flee from him as an injured animal might make a dash for safety to lick its wounds. But her feet seemed to be welded to the floor and she could not move. As they stared at each other she was conscious of an ache low in her pelvis and the slick warmth between her thighs added to her humiliation that he might detect the betraying musky scent of her arousal.

'Good morning.' A female voice came from the doorway. 'Oh! I apologise if I am interrupting…' the woman said as Savannah hastily stepped back from Dimitris.

'Good morning, Tara.' His tone was casual, and his features that seconds earlier had looked as though they were carved from granite took on a bland expression as he greeted the woman who had entered the studio. 'You are not interrupting anything. But if you had arrived a couple of minutes ago you would have seen me accidentally spill pancake batter everywhere. Miss O'Neal was helping to clear up the mess.'

'O'Neal?' A frown appeared on Tara Brown's perfectly made-up face. She was the epitome of elegance in a pale grey trouser suit and matching stiletto heels.

Savannah wished she'd worn heels instead of trainers. Out of habit she ran her fingers through her hair before remembering she'd tied it in a ponytail, which came loose so that blonde strands fell across her face. She thought she heard Dimitris make a rough noise in his throat.

'I just tried calling you to let you know that a problem has arisen with the photoshoot,' Tara Brown told him.

Savannah's heart sank as she waited for Dimitris to denounce her. But, to her surprise, he slipped his phone that still bore traces of batter mixture into the back pocket of his jeans.

'I dropped my phone earlier and it doesn't appear to be working,' he murmured. 'Give me a couple of minutes to change my shirt and then you can explain the situation.' He nodded to Tara and did not look at Savannah as he swung round and strode to the far end of the studio to disappear through a doorway.

The team of production assistants were arriving. Bright, confident professionals who were chatting and laughing as if they did not have a care in the world, Savannah thought enviously. She was certain that Dimitris would tell Tara Brown what she had done to his phone, and in all honesty she could not blame him. Her career as a food photographer was effectively over as a result of her stupid behaviour. No one wanted a diva on a photoshoot. Her common sense belatedly put in an appearance, and she decided to slink away and avoid an embarrassing conversation with Philpot's PR executive.

Dimitris slammed the door of his office that doubled up as a dressing room when his cooking programmes were filmed at the kitchen studio. He headed into the adjoining shower room, threw his shirt into the laundry basket and braced his hands on the vanity unit. Resting his forehead on the cool tiles above the sink, he dragged oxygen into his lungs.

*Damn her.*

The previous evening's unexpected encounter with Savannah had disturbed him sufficiently that he'd taken steps to prevent a second meeting today. But evidently she hadn't been informed by the photographic agency that she was not required for the photoshoot. When he'd spotted Savannah in the garden he had been dismayed by his body's reaction to her.

Among his friends it was a joke that the media had labelled him the Hot Chef. The nickname was a tongue-in-cheek reference to his sex appeal rather than his temperament. In fact he was renowned for his coolness under pressure. Nothing fazed him. Working in professional kitchens was a notoriously stressful environment, but Dimitris always remained calm. However, meeting Savannah again had evoked a primitive response in him.

He pictured her in slim-fitting black trousers and a stretchy tee shirt that showed off her toned figure and those firm breasts that he'd glimpsed rather more of last night when they had spilled out of the front of her dress. When he'd found Savannah in a hotel room with his would-be brother-in-law she had looked like a seductress in her sexy dress. Dimitris told himself he could not be blamed for his assumption that she was Matt Collier's mistress. But she had insisted that she hadn't known Collier was engaged to Eleni. Ten years ago Savannah had been fiercely honest.

*'Maybe you don't love me, but you can't stop me feeling the way I do about you. I love you, Dimitris.'*

Cursing the unwanted memories of his relationship with a teenage Savannah that Dimitris had known from the start was a mistake, he strode across to the wardrobe and took out a clean shirt. In truth, the real reason he had asked Philpot's to arrange for a different photographer was because he'd wanted to avoid the edgy feeling Savannah aroused in him.

It was not the only thing she aroused, he thought self-derisively. He had been uncomfortably hard from the moment he'd found her in the garden, looking entirely too beautiful and still with that air of vulnerability that tugged on his protective instincts. Unfortunately, those instincts had not been apparent when he'd almost kissed her.

Dimitris did not know what disturbed him most—that he'd been overwhelmed by an urgent desire to cover Savannah's mouth with his, or that he'd come to his senses in time and pulled back. The flare of disappointment in her hazel-green eyes had nearly tempted him to take her in his arms again, and to hell with the consequences.

But he'd had to deal with the consequences of his actions on that fateful car journey eighteen years ago. He bitterly regretted his hot-headedness when he had been a teenager. Emotions were dangerous, which was why he channelled his passion into cooking, and why he never allowed any woman too close.

*'You are an empty shell,'* one of his ex-lovers had accused him, when inevitably he'd ended the relationship after a few weeks.

Women had fallen for him since he was a youth, and more so since he'd become wealthy, he acknowledged cynically. What would they say if he told them that he was toxic? He had killed his parents and ruined his sister's life. How would Savannah react if he admitted the truth? He had never told her anything about the car accident. He'd never spoken to anyone about what had happened and his belief that it had been his fault.

Dimitris's jaw clenched. He was unlikely to ever

see Savannah again. For years she had hovered on the periphery of his consciousness. He had convinced himself that he remembered her because she was the only virgin he'd slept with. He preferred his lovers to be experienced and his no-strings rule was non-negotiable.

He switched on his phone and cursed when the screen remained blank. Savannah's outrageous behaviour when she'd dropped his phone into the batter mixture had fired his temper, and in those moments of heightened emotion a mixture of anger and desire had seen him pull her into his arms. Thank God he'd come to his senses before he had kissed her.

The young woman he had known years ago had been sweet and shy and had adored him with a puppy-like devotion that Dimitris had been bitterly aware he did not deserve. This new Savannah had an attitude and a temper. She was even more beautiful and decidedly sassier than she'd been at eighteen, and she tested his self-control like no other woman ever had.

Determinedly shoving the past back where it belonged, Dimitris returned to the studio and found his assistants and technicians setting up for the photoshoot. Philpot's PR executive Tara Brown looked tense.

'The agency sent another photographer instead of Savannah O'Neal, as you requested,' she explained.

'There seems to be some confusion about why Miss O'Neal came to the studio today. Unfortunately, her replacement was involved in an accident on his way here and has been taken to hospital. I am trying to arrange another photographer, but I'm afraid it means a delay to the start of the photoshoot. The alternative is to postpone until another day.'

Dimitris did not favour delaying the shoot. His sister had flown to Athens that morning, in need of sympathy from a friend who was to have been her chief bridesmaid. He was keen to return to Rhodes and break the news to his grandmother that the wedding was cancelled before Eleni arrived at the villa. *Γιαγιά* Hestia's well-meant fussing would be too much for his sister right now.

The solution to get back on track was obvious, but he was reluctant to suggest that Savannah could take the photographs. He had a curious feeling that his life was about to change for ever. Impatiently, he reminded himself that he was in control of his destiny. His reaction to Savannah, *that near-kiss*, had stemmed from his shock at seeing her again.

'Rather than delay the shoot, you could ask Miss O'Neal to take the photos for the magazine. I might have acted too hastily when I asked for a different photographer.' He correctly interpreted Tara Brown's confused expression. 'I've had a second look at Miss O'Neal's portfolio and decided that I like her style of photography.'

Tara did not hide her relief. 'I saw her leave the studio a few minutes ago. I'll go after her.'

'She can't have got far.' Dimitris glanced at his watch. 'The shoot is already behind schedule, and we need to make a start.'

He was puzzled by Savannah's claim that she needed the Philpot's assignment. It couldn't be for financial reasons. When she'd turned twenty-five she should have come into a great deal of money that had been held in a trust fund managed by her father.

He recalled, with a mixture of bitterness and distaste, the meeting he'd had with Savannah's father ten years ago. The offer of money as a bribe had been humiliating. But he'd been persuaded to break off his relationship with Savannah to protect her fortune after Richard O'Neal had threatened to remove her as a beneficiary of the trust fund and cut her off financially. Dimitris wasn't proud that he'd accepted the money, but he had done so to prevent Savannah learning the truth about Richard.

Fate had conspired to throw them together again, he brooded. But he only had to get through today, and thankfully his emotions were back under control. Although the uncomfortable throb in his groin when Savannah walked into the studio a few minutes later mocked his belief that he was unaffected by her.

# CHAPTER FOUR

'MISS O'NEAL...'

Savannah heard a voice behind her and slowly turned around to see Philpot's PR executive hurrying down the driveway. She braced herself for a showdown, convinced that Dimitris must have made a formal complaint about her behaviour.

'Thank goodness you hadn't left. We want you to stay for the photoshoot after all.' Tara Brown sounded flustered. 'The other photographer sent by the agency can't make it. Apparently he fell down the escalator at the tube station and has a suspected broken wrist.'

'Mr Kyriakou won't want to work with me,' Savannah said with certainty. Not because she had stupidly damaged his phone, but because Dimitris had wanted to kiss her. The self-disgust in his eyes when he'd set her away from him had heaped more humiliation on her.

'It was Dimitris's idea to call you back.'

Savannah wondered if the replacement photographer had really been involved in an accident. Perhaps Dimitris had set her up to humiliate her publicly for her unprofessional behaviour. But if there was any chance she could salvage her career and professional reputation she would be a fool not to take it. Still she hesitated, reluctant to face Dimitris again. It would be safer on her emotions if she walked away.

'Miss O'Neal?' the PR woman prompted.

'Okay,' Savannah said quickly before she could change her mind. She needed the money, and all she had to do was work with Dimitris for one day. 'I'll stay for the shoot.'

Her heart thumped as she followed Tara Brown across the garden, and she took a deep breath before she stepped into the studio. The oxygen escaped from Savannah's lungs in a whoosh when the first person she saw, the only person she saw in fact, even though the room was full of people, was Dimitris.

Her gaze collided with his and she noticed that his eyes were the same shade of navy-blue as the shirt he'd changed into after she'd wiped batter over him. The top couple of buttons were undone to reveal a vee of olive-gold skin and a sprinkling of black chest hairs. He was lethally beautiful, and it occurred to her that she might not survive him a second time.

For a split-second she was tempted to run back to her car and break the speed limit driving away from Richmond. Food photography entailed working in close proximity to the creator of the dishes. She would have to stand beside Dimitris and photograph each stage of him preparing his recipes, but how on earth would she be able to hide her treacherous body's response to him?

'Miss O'Neal. Savannah. Welcome to River Retreat studio,' Dimitris greeted her smoothly. He glanced around at his assistants, mostly young women who gazed at him like adoring concubines in the presence of their sultan. 'We have a busy day ahead, but before we get down to business I prepared breakfast for everyone. Help yourself to Greek style pancakes with honey and walnuts. I made a fresh batch of pancake batter,' he added drily when Savannah sent him a startled look.

She felt herself blush as an assistant pushed a serving plate across the counter towards her. The thick, fluffy pancakes drizzled with golden honey and sprinkled with crushed walnuts looked divine, but although she was hungry her stomach rebelled at the idea of putting food into it. She doubted she'd ever look at a pancake again without cringing with embarrassment.

She unpacked her camera equipment and read through the schedule of dishes that she would be photographing. The art director and food stylist introduced themselves and discussed ideas for props to be used in the shoot. Dimitris strolled over to join in the conversation and Savannah hoped he did not notice her stiffen as she struggled to ignore her awareness of him.

'Thank you for giving me the chance to prove the quality of my work,' she murmured after the stylist and director had walked away.

'It makes sense for you to do the photoshoot as you are already here. I don't have time for a delay.' Dimitris's jaw hardened. 'I must go to Greece to support my sister.'

Savannah remembered how caring and protective he had been of Eleni years ago. She had even felt envious that he loved his sister but not her. From his curt tone she guessed he still blamed her for Eleni's broken engagement. Her temper simmered. She couldn't work with Dimitris while she was conscious of his disapproval.

'Is Eleni very upset?'

'What do you think?'

'I think Matt Collier made a fool of us both, and I also think Eleni could do better than to marry a cheat and liar.'

Dimitris stared at her, and Savannah thought she saw an imperceptible softening of his hard features that gave her hope he was prepared to believe she had been duped by Matt to have a relationship with him.

'Tell me about your methods for photographing food,' he said, breaking the tense silence between them. 'I see you use a DSLR.'

'A digital single-lens reflex camera allows me to shoot a lot of pictures fast so that I can capture every detail of a dish as it is being created. I'll take literally hundreds of shots to achieve the perfect image. Speed is of the essence,' Savannah explained as she warmed to her theme. 'I've discovered that it only takes seconds before a bowl of pasta loses its glossiness and looks dry, and crisp lettuce leaves adorned with a creamy dressing soon wilt and appear unappealing.'

He nodded. 'I agree that food must look so real it almost leaps off the page. When readers look at photographs in a magazine, rather than see inanimate pictures I want their senses to be fired so that they imagine the aroma of spicy lamb koftas and the crispy texture of filo pastry.' He glanced at his watch. 'There is a lot to do. I hope you're prepared for a long day.'

She followed Dimitris over to the kitchen island and watched him assemble the ingredients for the first dish he would cook. He moved with an easy grace and once again she was struck by how incredibly handsome he was. It was no surprise that he was a sex symbol to his legions of female fans. But Savannah was determined to ignore her inconvenient attraction to him and concentrate on the job that gave her the means to financially support her mum and pay for the care Evelyn needed as her MS worsened.

Tears pricked her eyes. Her mum was the sweetest, kindest person. Gentle and unworldly, Evelyn had been an art therapist who had devoted her time to helping others until her illness had forced her to give up work and she was no longer able to paint. Savannah would do anything for her mum, even if it meant working with the man who had once broken her heart. After today she would not have to see Dimitris again, but meanwhile her camera felt comfortably familiar in her hands as she started to shoot.

Hours later Savannah stretched, her muscles tight from standing for long periods of time and aiming her camera. She hitched herself onto a stool in front of the counter and opened her laptop to download the last batch of photographs. It would take her a few days to edit the pictures before sending them to the team at Philpot's. The art director and Dimitris would have the final say on which photos would appear in the magazine.

The photoshoot had been fast-paced and hectic, and she'd discovered that Dimitris was a consummate professional. He was a talented and passionate chef, and his recipes were innovative yet unfussy. Savannah had worked with many chefs since she'd become a food photographer, including some who were full of their own self-importance and strutted around the kitchen like demi-gods, shouting orders at their hapless assistants.

Dimitris was relaxed and charming, and he'd worked tirelessly throughout the long day to produce twelve different dishes—most chefs would make four or five. He'd insisted that the production team took breaks to eat the food once it had been photographed, but Savannah had been too engrossed in her work and had only drunk a couple of cups of coffee all day.

The awkwardness she'd felt with Dimitris had disappeared while they'd worked together. He had been keen for her to take unusual shots—a close-up of a mussel, a garlic clove at the moment it was crushed beneath the blade of a knife, spaghetti sliding out of the pan and falling messily onto a plate.

'I'm looking for authenticity in the photos,' he explained. 'Food shouldn't be perfectly arranged on a plate. Real food is honest and sexy, and I want images that make people drool.'

The dishes he created were a feast for the senses, and his energy and enthusiasm made him the most exciting chef Savannah had ever worked with. The photographs she had taken were some of her best, even to her perfectionist eyes. Looking up from her laptop some while later, she discovered that she was alone. The production team had packed up the lighting equipment and props and the kitchen assistants had cleared away the mountain of pots and pans. The studio was peaceful, bathed in the golden sunlight of a summer's evening.

Dimitris emerged from his dressing room. Evidently he'd just showered, and his hair was still damp and curled rebelliously over his collar. He had changed his clothes again and was wearing a white silk shirt and narrow black trousers that from their superb tailoring were doubtless a designer brand. Everything about the way he looked spoke of a successful self-made multi-millionaire who had reached the pinnacle of his career and was comfortable in his own skin.

He stood behind Savannah and looked over her shoulder at the photos on her laptop screen. 'These are very good.'

'They'll be better after I've edited them.' She breathed in the citrus and spice scent of his cologne and felt a tug deep in her pelvis. 'I hadn't noticed how late it is. I'm sure you want to rush back to Greece to comfort your sister. Eleni must be devastated that her marriage plans have been ruined.'

'At least she discovered that Matt Collier is an unreliable cheat before she married him,' Dimitris said evenly. 'Eleni called to say she is going to stay with friends in Santorini for a few days and I am not in a rush to return to Rhodes.'

'I expect you have plans for the evening.' The

tabloids had recently been in a frenzy after Dimitris was spotted leaving a nightclub with an actress from a popular TV soap. Savannah felt a stab of jealousy. She was desperate to leave before he guessed how much he still affected her. She packed up her laptop and slid off the stool, but an agonising sensation of pins and needles in her foot made her legs buckle.

Dimitris caught hold of her arm as she stumbled. 'Are you all right?' He cursed. 'I'm not surprised that you almost fainted. You didn't eat anything all day.'

'I'm fine.' She prayed he did not notice the frantic thud of her pulse in her wrist.

He clearly wasn't convinced. 'You can't drive home while you are feeling lightheaded. You had better stay for dinner.'

Savannah bit her lip. Dimitris had sounded far from enthusiastic. 'Three's a crowd. I assumed you have a date tonight,' she mumbled when he raised an eyebrow.

'I don't,' he said drily.

She looked away from his enigmatic gaze and saw a white stain down the front of her black tee shirt. The likely culprit was yoghurt. A tub had been spilt over the worktop and must have transferred to her clothes when she'd leaned in to take a close-up shot of a dish of moussaka with a yoghurt and cheese topping.

'You can freshen up at the house. Besides, we still need to discuss what you intend to do about replacing my phone.' He picked up her camera bag. 'Can you walk, or do you still feel faint?'

'I'm fine. It was just a cramp in my foot.' Common sense told her to decline his offer of dinner, but the microwavable meal waiting for her at home did not hold much appeal, and the opportunity to see inside his home was irresistible.

'My housekeeper Mary and her husband John look after the house and garden,' Dimitris explained when they left the studio and walked along a path lined with lavender bushes and roses. The perfume of the flowers was intoxicating in the sultry air of the summer's evening. The recent heatwave was forecast to end with thunderstorms.

'John also drives me when I need a chauffeur. Did you park in the road?' Savannah nodded. 'Give me your keys and John will move your car onto the driveway.'

He ushered her through a set of French windows into an elegant drawing room with a parquet floor. 'When the previous owners renovated the house they kept many of the original Victorian features,' Dimitris explained, watching Savannah trace her fingers over the oak panels that lined the walls.

She followed him into a huge entrance hall with an exquisite tiled floor. 'You have a beautiful house and an amazingly successful career. Did you ever imagine when you lived in a flat above your grandfather's restaurant that you would be a famous chef and would own a property in an expensive part of London?'

'Yes.' His chiselled features showed no emotion. 'I was always ambitious and knew where I wanted to be. I never doubted I would be successful.'

Dimitris had put his pursuit of success above everything else—including her. Savannah had always known it, but his stark admission did not hurt any less. His determination to establish his career had been at the expense of their relationship, such as it had been. She supposed he had used the money her father had given him to open his first restaurant in Greece.

The truth was that at eighteen she had been too young to fall in love. She had been looking for affection that her father had denied her, and she'd mistaken her teenage fascination with Dimitris for a deeper emotion. It infuriated her that she hadn't forgotten him in ten years. But she was an adult now and meeting him again was an opportunity to realise that he was not a fairy tale prince but an ordinary man with flaws, and she hoped she would finally be able to get over him.

The woman who Savannah had met when she'd arrived at River Retreat that morning emerged from the kitchen. 'Ah, Mary,' Dimitris greeted her. 'Can you show Miss O'Neal to the guest cloakroom.

She will be staying for dinner. We'll eat outside on the deck.'

A few minutes later Savannah groaned when she saw her reflection in the cloakroom mirror. Her ponytail had come loose, and she had panda eyes where her mascara had smudged in the heat of the studio lights. She ran her fingers through her choppy shoulder-length bob. When she had worked as a cosmetics model she'd been advised by a make-up artist to always keep in her handbag eyeliner and a rose-coloured lip gloss that doubled up as blusher, to highlight her cheekbones.

A voice came from the hall. 'Miss O'Neal, I've brought you something to wear.' Savannah opened the door and saw the housekeeper holding a pile of colourful silks. 'Dimitris often hosts pool parties, and these kaftan dresses are for female guests if they want to cover up after swimming,' Mary explained. 'He suggested you might want to get changed and I'll launder your clothes while you are having dinner.'

Savannah remembered in the magazine article about Dimitris there had been a photo of the swimming pool, which was a modern addition in the basement of the house. He had been pictured sprawled on a poolside lounger, surrounded by gorgeous women wearing tiny bikinis and not a kaftan in sight.

Back in the cloakroom, she stripped off her

stained tee shirt and trousers. Sifting through the kaftans, she picked one made of pale gold silk. The flowing gown felt deliciously cool on her skin, and the golden threads woven through the material glimmered softly when she moved.

She tied the matching belt around her waist and slipped off her trainers, deciding to go barefoot. For a final touch she took her perfume spritzer from her handbag and sprayed her neck and wrists with her favourite fragrance. The scent evoked memories of her eighteenth birthday party.

It nearly hadn't happened after her parents had been delayed by a tropical cyclone in Asia and were unable to fly home in time for her birthday. Her mother had persuaded her father to allow the party to go ahead. The sense of freedom had been heady when Savannah had woken on the day she turned eighteen, an adult free to make her own choices. Her first attempt to be more independent when she'd got a job as a waitress at Dimitris's grandfather's restaurant had not won her father's approval as she'd hoped. He had said that Hestia's restaurant in a run-down area of London was not the kind of place he expected his daughter to work. Savannah had felt that she could never please her father.

The party that evening had been on the terrace next to the outdoor pool. The party organisers had set up a champagne bar in the pool house and the caterers had served canapés. Savannah remembered that she had laughed and danced and given the impression that she was having a wonderful time. But as the hours had passed and *he* hadn't arrived, she'd wanted to cry with disappointment.

'Dimitris is working this evening,' Eleni had told her when in a fiercely casual voice Savannah had asked if he was coming to the party. 'The private function was booked at the last minute. My grandfather said we need the money and Dimitris must cook tonight, even though Hestia's is usually closed on Sundays.'

Eleni had tired easily and needed to go home early. Savannah had wheeled her chair out to the car when her grandfather came to collect her. The party had palled after Eleni had left, and she'd been relieved when the other guests departed at eleven o'clock, leaving behind the debris of balloons and banners and birthday cake squashed onto the patio stones. She'd kicked off her high heels and sat on the side of the pool to dip her toes in the water when a deep voice over her shoulder caused her pulse to skyrocket...

'Happy birthday, Savannah.'

Dimitris emerged from the shadows, and she scrambled to her feet, staring at him with her heart in her eyes. 'You came,' she said breathlessly.

'I said I would.' He gave a wry smile. 'Better late than never.'

There was still an hour left of her birthday and

Dimitris's arrival made it the best birthday ever. She smiled at him, and the low sound he made in his throat sent a quiver of excitement through her. It occurred to her that she'd only ever seen him at the restaurant when she answered the service bell or carried dirty plates to the sink. Her shy overtures and his playful flirting had taken place in a busy kitchen. This was the first time she'd been alone with him.

'I have never seen you look as beautiful as you do tonight.' Dimitris had only ever seen her wearing a waitress's uniform. Savannah had spent hours choosing a dress for the party, and she hoped the silver halter-neck gown would make him realise that she wasn't a foolish girl. She was a woman with needs that only he could fulfil.

'This is for you,' he said huskily. 'Your birthday present.'

She took the package he held out and ripped off the brightly coloured wrapping paper to reveal a bottle of perfume. Sensuelle, the new fragrance by a famous perfume house, was exorbitantly expensive.

'Thank you, but you shouldn't have...' she faltered, blushing at her clumsiness.

'I won't always be poor,' he drawled. There was steel beneath his soft tone. 'Allow me.' He unscrewed the lid on the bottle and tipped a few drops of perfume onto his fingertip. 'Move your hair.'

Mesmerised by him, she lifted her hair and he

pressed his finger to the sensitive spot behind her ear, transferring the exquisite fragrance to her skin. Her heart thudded as Dimitris trailed his fingers over her neck and collarbone, hovered over the pulse beating erratically at the base of her throat, before sliding down her décolletage to the vee between her breasts.

'You've driven me crazy for weeks.' His hoarse admission made her feel dizzy with desire and when he drew her into his arms she tilted her face up to his and parted her lips for his kiss. Dimitris's eyes were the inky blue of the night sky and gleamed as brightly as the stars. 'I want to make love to you, *mátia mou*.'

She pressed herself closer to him, eager to become a woman and give her body to the man who had captured her heart. 'I want you too.'

Swallowing hard, Savannah jerked her mind back to the present. Ten years ago she had been young and in love. She'd naively believed that Dimitris felt the same way about her—although he'd never actually said that he loved her, she thought with a heavy sigh.

When she stepped out of the cloakroom the housekeeper was waiting for her and led the way through the house and across the garden. Dimitris was standing on the deck, half turned towards the river. Savannah's heart missed a beat as she studied his proud profile. He was gorgeous—and unobtainable. She understood now what she'd refused to accept at eighteen, when her heart had been full of hope and her head full of dreams.

Anger seared her with the white heat of a lightning bolt. She was furious with herself for being so affected by Dimitris. How pathetic that she only wore the brand of perfume he had given her for a birthday present *ten years ago* as some kind of homage to him. She was twenty-eight and he was the only man she had slept with. She was mired in the past, trapped by the immature feelings she'd once had for Dimitris. It was time, way past time in fact, that she moved on and stopped being an idiot over a playboy who probably hadn't given her a second thought in years.

# CHAPTER FIVE

DIMITRIS SENSED SAVANNAH'S presence behind him although she hadn't made a sound. The evocative fragrance she wore was carried towards him on the faint breeze, evoking memories he had never managed to forget and rousing his body to instant and urgent life.

There had been occasions in the past decade when he'd been in a nightclub or bar somewhere in the world and caught a hint of perfume that he recognised as Sensuelle, and had found himself transported back in time to a balmy summer's night in a north London suburb.

By the time he'd finished work at the restaurant he'd known that Savannah's party would have ended. If he'd had any sense he would not have jumped on his motorbike and ridden to her parents' mansion on the edge of Hampstead Heath. But then if he'd had any sense he would not have spent far more of his wages than he could afford on perfume for her birthday present.

All summer he had been enchanted by Savannah's shy smile. She'd made him think he could be a better person than he knew he was, and even that he might one day be able to forgive himself for destroying his family. It had been a difficult summer, with worries about his grandfather's failing health and his sister's latest round of surgery. Savannah had been a distraction from his responsibilities and the guilt that hung like a dark shadow over him.

His grandfather would have retired years before if Dimitris's father had been alive to take over the restaurant. Likewise, if the accident hadn't happened Eleni would have been able to go dancing, but instead she was stuck in a wheelchair while her schoolfriends had fun. Only Savannah hadn't abandoned her friend, and her loyalty had forged a strong bond between the two girls.

Dimitris had been aware of Savannah's fascination with him. It was not the first time it had happened, and previously with other young women he had gently but firmly made it clear that he wasn't interested. He should not have got involved with Savannah and he certainly should not have made love to her on a daybed in the pool house, especially after she'd confirmed his suspicion that she was a virgin.

Cursing beneath his breath, he jerked his mind away from the past. But there was danger in the present, he realised as he raked his gaze over Savannah and felt an urge to spear his fingers in her messily sexy blonde hair.

All day he had been supremely conscious of her standing close to him in the studio while she'd taken photos of the food he'd cooked. Her svelte figure revealed by her tight-fitting clothes had driven him to distraction. It should be a relief that she had changed into a loose kaftan that concealed rather than flaunted her feminine shape. But the shimmering silk skimmed her body and gave a hint of the delectable curves beneath it.

For years whenever Dimitris had detected the heady scent of dark red roses mixed with the sweetness of peonies and the smoky warmth of the exotic essential oil Oudh that a perfumier had combined to create Sensuelle, he had instinctively looked for Savannah and felt unsettled by his disappointment that she was not there. She was here now, and he was conscious of the heavy thud of his pulse when she came to stand beside him on the deck.

He pulled out a chair for her to sit down at the table and knew from the imperceptible stiffening of her body that she felt the electrical current that passed between them.

'Your car wouldn't start,' he told her as he moved round the table and sat opposite her. 'John thinks it might need a new battery. He'll arrange for the car to be towed to a garage in the morning so that it can be checked by a mechanic.' He uncorked the wine. 'At least you can have a drink. John will drive you home later.'

She seemed about to decline, but then gave a shrug. 'Why not. It's been quite a day.'

He poured the wine and lifted his glass towards her. 'To unexpected reunions,' he murmured drily.

Dimitris had chosen a robust red made from a variety of grapes called Xinomavro that were grown on the wine estates in northern Greece. There was an earthiness to the wine, yet it was surprisingly smooth. Savannah took a sip from her glass and gave a faint sigh as she visibly relaxed.

'This looks amazing,' she murmured, studying the platters of food on the table when Dimitris removed the covers.

There were colourful salads, dolmades—vine leaves stuffed with rice and herbs, meatballs with feta cheese, grilled Halloumi served with wedges of lemon and plump Kalamata olives.

'Mezze is my favourite kind of meal,' he admitted as he passed her various dishes. 'I think of it as honest food made from simple ingredients, but created with care and passion it becomes a feast. Sharing food with friends is one of life's fundamental pleasures.'

Cooking was much more than his career. It was an outlet for his creativity and allowed him to deal with emotions that he kept under tight control in every other area of his life and relationships.

Savannah tucked in enthusiastically. 'Everything is delicious,' she said as she tore off a piece of pitta bread, dipped it into a bowl of creamy hummus and popped the morsel into her mouth. 'And messy.' Her tongue darted out to lick hummus from her fingers. Catching Dimitris's gaze, she gave him an impish smile. 'I haven't discovered an elegant way to eat with my fingers.'

Elegant be damned. His blood roared in his ears. Earlier he had been reminded of how tactile Savannah was when he'd watched her stroke her fingers over the wooden panels in the drawing room. He had imagined her touching him and learning his body anew. Now he felt an overwhelming urge to stride around the table and pull her into his arms so that he could flick his tongue over the corner of her mouth and lick off the tiny smear of hummus. He wanted to taste the red wine that stained her lips. But overwhelmed was not a word in his vocabulary. It suggested a loss of control, and he never allowed that to happen.

He forced his mind from the carnal thoughts that he reminded himself were inappropriate when he'd already decided he would not see Savannah again after this evening. But he was curious about her and steered the conversation to safer topics.

'What made you decide to work behind a camera rather than in front of it?'

'I suppose you are referring to my brief modelling

career.' This time her smile was self-deprecating. 'It wasn't something I set out to do. After university I got a job with a web design company.'

'I remember you had planned to study art at university.' It was disturbing that he had not forgotten anything about her, Dimitris brooded. Savannah had made an impact on him in a way that no other woman ever had.

'I switched to fine art photography. But I found working in web design didn't really interest me. When I was spotted by a modelling agency and won a contract to represent a cosmetics company it gave me a new direction and the opportunity to travel and meet some interesting people.'

'Why did you stop?'

'My mum fell ill, and I moved back home to help look after her.' Savannah drank the rest of her wine, and Dimitris leaned across the table to refill her glass. 'When Mum was first diagnosed with multiple sclerosis she was still able to work in her garden that she loved so much. For fun I started playing around taking photos of the vegetables she'd grown and the meals we made from home produced ingredients. I put together a series of photographs for a calendar to raise funds for the MS charity. That led to my interest in food photography. Being a freelance photographer allows me to arrange my work so that I'm at home when Mum's carer has a day off.'

She sighed. 'The downside of being self-employed is that I don't earn a regular salary and it's taking a while to establish myself as a food photographer. I hope my car won't be too expensive to fix because I can't afford a big repair bill…or buy you a new phone.'

Dimitris was annoyed at the inconvenience of having to replace the phone that Savannah had destroyed, but he was even more irritated that she'd blatantly lied. 'You must have had a wild time for the last three years to have spent the substantial amount of money in your trust fund,' he drawled.

She looked puzzled. 'How do you know I was supposed to receive a lot of money when I turned twenty-five? When we knew each other ten years ago I was unaware that my father had created a trust fund and made me the beneficiary.'

Dimitris silently cursed his mistake in mentioning the trust fund that Richard O'Neal had spoken of when he'd blackmailed him to end his relationship with Savannah by threatening to cut off financial support for her. 'You said you were *supposed* to receive the money. Why didn't you?'

She lifted her glass and drank more wine before replying. 'Three years ago my father was suspected of financial impropriety. Following a lengthy police investigation he was charged and later convicted of serious fraud. His assets were seized, including money that he'd placed in a trust fund. I was meant to be the beneficiary, but my father, who was the sole trustee, had established the fund to launder money he'd acquired through his corrupt business dealings. Obviously I didn't have a legal right to the fund that was used to conceal my father's criminal activities.'

While they had been eating, dusk had fallen and the solar lamps on the deck cast long shadows. 'Two months ago my father died, owing several million pounds,' Savannah continued tonelessly. 'At the end of his trial he was found guilty and given a five-year prison sentence. His outstanding legal bill and other debts must be paid out of his estate, and there will be nothing left for my mum to live on.'

*'Theós!'* Dimitris was stunned by the news of Richard O'Neal's death, and the realisation that the other man had taken the details of their private conversation to his grave. He gathered that Richard hadn't told Savannah he was not in fact her father. From what Savannah had said, Dimitris guessed her mother had not explained the truth. It was not his place to reveal the secret that was likely to be devastating for Savannah, but he felt uncomfortable. 'What about Pond House?' he asked.

'It will have to be sold to pay back everything my father owed. I haven't had the heart to tell my mum how bad the situation really is. She loves Pond House. I would do anything to keep it, but I can't see a way. Mum doesn't have any money of her own and I've spent virtually all of my savings on the upkeep of the house and private nursing care for her.'

Savannah gave a hollow laugh. 'It's a pity I didn't marry Hugo Roxwell when I had the chance. At least I would have been entitled to the sizeable divorce settlement which was included in the prenuptial agreement Hugo had wanted me to sign.'

When Dimitris had seen a photo of Savannah smiling at her English aristocrat and showing off a diamond engagement ring he'd felt sick to his stomach. The newspaper had reported that the happy couple were planning a lavish wedding at the country estate of Hugo's father, Lord Roxwell.

For three days Dimitris had drunk himself into a stupor, but then he'd sobered up and focused on building his career, and if occasionally he'd imagined Savannah happily married and with a brood of children, he'd reminded himself that he did not deserve to have a wife and a family of his own. He wondered why she hadn't married.

'I take it that the path of true love did not run smoothly. You didn't waste any time after we had broken up, accepting a marriage proposal from your aristocrat boyfriend.'

She glared at him. 'I think I can be forgiven for being flattered by Hugo's attention after the way you treated me. You told me on the day I was flying to New York for a belated birthday trip with my parents that our relationship was over. When

I arrived home four days later, the restaurant was boarded up and a neighbour told me that you had moved to Greece with your grandparents and sister.'

Her voice was unsteady. 'Eleni was my best friend, but I didn't get a chance to say goodbye to her. She sent a text saying that you had told her not to keep in contact with me. That was cruel. Even if you hated me, you had no right to spoil my friendship with Eleni.'

'I didn't hate you,' Dimitris muttered. He could not explain that Richard O'Neal had insisted on severing all ties. 'I suppose your father approved of your aristocrat.'

She nodded. 'My father had come from a poor background, and he was obsessed with status and climbing the social ladder. He put pressure on me to marry well. He'd invested money in an art gallery owned by Lord Roxwell and managed by Hugo. My father arranged for me to work as an assistant at the gallery and persuaded me to defer my place at university for a year.'

Savannah sighed. 'Hugo was charming and attentive. The truth is that I was on the rebound after you had dumped me, and I convinced myself that I had feelings for Hugo. But I realised that I wasn't ready for marriage. When I suggested to Hugo that we should wait for a year or two, he was furious. He admitted he'd wanted a rushed wedding because his grandmother's will stated that he had to be married before he could claim the inheritance she had left him. Hugo moaned that his father gave him a pittance for an allowance.'

Her hazel-green eyes glowed with angry fire. 'Hugo was only interested in money, and he wasn't in love with me. I seem to attract men who don't care about me. You didn't,' she said bitterly.

In fact he had begun to have feelings for Savannah ten years ago, Dimitris brooded. He'd been terrified that he could actually fall in love with her. Love was a responsibility he did not want. In his head he had still been a grief-stricken fourteen-year-old boy. Supposing he caused an accident and Savannah died, just as his parents had died? He could not bear to lose someone else he loved. He had decided when he was a teenager that it was safer not to allow love into his life, and it was a rule he'd kept for the past eighteen years. But he owed Savannah some sort of explanation.

'I accepted money from your father because my grandfather was seriously ill and desperate to return to Rhodes. My grandparents had spent what little money they had on caring for my sister and I after our parents were killed. The money allowed me to buy a house in the village where my grandfather had been born so that he and my grandmother could retire, and it was where he died two years later.'

Savannah stood up and walked to the edge of the deck. For a few moments she stared at the dark river before she turned and leaned against the rail. The moon had risen and in its silvery gleam she was mystical and insanely beautiful. Dimitris could not look away from her. In the distance came the rumble of thunder that warned of a gathering storm.

'You put a financial value on me when I was eighteen and made me feel worthless. You took my pride and my heart and trampled on them.'

His jaw clenched when he heard the pain in her voice. He felt guilty that he'd hurt her, but he could not explain that one reason he'd accepted money from Richard O'Neal had been to protect Savannah's financial security. It was ironic that despite his good intentions and his belief that he had acted in Savannah's best interest, she and her mother had been left penniless as a result of Richard's criminal activities.

'I can understand that you'd wanted to help your grandfather. It must have been an easy decision to accept money from my father because you never loved me,' she said, still in that brittle voice that felt like a knife in his chest. 'But there is something you want from me, isn't there, Dimitris?'

He wanted to deny it, but his heart gave a jolt when Savannah untied the belt of her kaftan. 'What are you doing?' he demanded.

She did not reply, and his breath hissed between his teeth as he watched her lift the gold silk gown over her head in a fluid movement and drop it onto the deck. Dimitris heard a harsh curse and realised it had come from him. Savannah's pale pink bra and knickers were not especially fancy, but somehow that made her even sexier.

'Put that goddamned thing back on.' He stared at the kaftan that was a pool of gold at her feet, not daring to look at a half-naked Savannah when he was imagining peeling her panties down her milky thighs. 'You are making a fool of yourself,' he bit out.

'I have been a fool over you for too long.' She walked back across the deck, a silver goddess dappled by moonlight.

Dimitris felt his blood thicken and head south to his sex as his eyes were drawn to the dark outline of her nipples visible beneath her lacy bra cups. He leaned back in his chair when she stood in front of him. For once she was taller than him and he had to look up at her face.

*Theós!* She was as exquisite as Aphrodite from ancient Greek legend. He felt a nerve flicker in his cheek as he fought to control his response to her. 'What do you think I want from you?'

She leaned towards him and placed her hands on his shoulders. Her breasts swung forwards and he clenched his fists to stop himself from cradling the plump mounds in his palms.

'This,' she whispered against his mouth.

And God help him, Dimitris could not deny

it. But he *must* resist Savannah. She was the only woman to have ever breached his defences and he could not risk getting close to her again. But knowing the danger did not lessen his craving.

She was such a fool. She should have known that challenging the iceman would result in her humiliation. Dimitris's hands lay on his thighs, and he made no attempt to touch her. His mouth was a rigid line beneath her lips and his eyes had narrowed so that Savannah had no idea what he was thinking. Only the laboured rise and fall of his chest gave a clue that he was not as unaffected as he wanted her to believe.

Frantic to evoke a reaction from him, she nipped his lower lip with her teeth. His lashes flew open and the hard glittering desire in his eyes caused her heart to miss a beat. Dimitris swore and clamped his hand to the back of her head as he opened his mouth beneath hers and the kiss exploded between them. *Finally.*

Savannah's limbs turned to jelly. She had initiated the kiss, but Dimitris took charge of it, sliding his lips over hers with thrilling mastery. A sudden loud clap of thunder sent shockwaves through her and raindrops as big as pennies spattered against the deck and lashed her skin.

Without breaking the kiss, Dimitris levered himself out of his chair and wrapped his arm around her waist to steady her. He towered over her, and she arched her neck while he continued kissing her and kissing her with a hunger that made her wonder if he had missed her through the long years apart as much as she had missed him. Of course he hadn't, her common sense piped up. He was responding in the same way that any male in the prime of his life would when a woman had thrown herself at him.

The rain was falling harder, and Dimitris's black curls were plastered to his brow. He caught hold of her hand and pulled her after him across the sodden lawn towards the house. Lamps had been switched on in the drawing room and their harsh brightness was an unwelcome return to reality after the concealing darkness outside.

Savannah felt the beginning of a headache that was probably the result of the wine. She only occasionally drank alcohol, and the wine had loosened her tongue and her inhibitions. But then Dimitris drew her into his arms, and she was only aware of him. His hands burned her skin and she ached for him to kiss her again until they were both ablaze in the inferno.

His midnight-dark eyes were as unfathomable as the deepest ocean. 'What do you want from me, Savannah?'

'One night with you. No strings and afterwards we walk away with no regrets.'

Her voice was surprisingly steady considering

her outrageous request. But she needed to do this. She was sure she remembered her very short affair with Dimitris through rose-coloured lenses. If she slept with him again she would realise that their relationship hadn't been the life-altering experience she'd let herself believe for all this time.

His expression was as enigmatic as always, but his hands gripped her waist harder, and she sensed his shock and something more primitive that made her heart kick in her chest. 'Why?'

'There is unfinished business between us. If you had stayed in London and we'd continued seeing each other perhaps our relationship would have petered out. But you left abruptly, and I couldn't forget you. You have been a splinter under my skin, and I want to be free of you.'

Dimitris raised an eyebrow. 'It's the first time I've been likened to a splinter.' His voice deepened and the hard glitter in his eyes sent a tremor through Savannah. 'But I agree we have unfinished business to resolve.' He stepped back from her and held out his hand. 'Come with me?'

Part of her wished he wasn't making it her choice. It would be easier if he swept her into his arms and carried her off to bed. But Savannah knew that this had to be her decision. When she put her fingers in his, the flare of hunger in Dimitris's eyes told her that beneath his coolness a fire raged. Without another word he tugged her after him out of the room and across the hall to the stairs.

She was breathless when they reached the second-floor landing, but from nervous excitement rather than exertion. His bedroom was overtly masculine with sleek, dark wood furnishings, a huge bed with a black leather headboard and, of all things, a mirror on the ceiling. Savannah tried not think of how many other women he must have made love to on the bed. Her face grew warm as she imagined herself and Dimitris lying on the satin sheets and looking up at the reflection of their naked bodies.

Anticipation and a sense of disbelief that this was happening and she was actually going to have sex with Dimitris made her feel strangely lightheaded.

'Savannah?' There was a question in his voice as if he thought she had changed her mind.

Keen to disabuse him of the idea, she put her hands on the front of his shirt and started to undo the buttons. Her fingers were shaking, and she took a deep breath. She didn't want Dimitris to guess that she was relatively inexperienced. 'You should get out of your wet clothes before you catch a chill.'

'There's not a chance of that happening. I'm burning up,' he said hoarsely when she spread his shirt open.

His skin felt like warm satin beneath her palms. The whorls of black hairs on his chest were thicker than she remembered. He had been handsome when he was younger, but now he was breathtaking, so big and male—and aroused, she discovered when he tumbled her down on the bed and lay beside her so that they were hip to hip. She felt the unmistakable bulge of his erection beneath his trousers.

Dimitris claimed her mouth in a kiss that was intensely erotic but also poignantly evocative of when they had been lovers all those years ago. Savannah couldn't stop shaking as she acknowledged the enormity of what she was about to do. Not to mention how enormous he was, she thought with slightly hysterical humour. Was she making a mistake?

Doubt swirled in the pit of her stomach. Should she tell him that she hadn't made love for ten years, and he was her only lover? But he might reject her if she admitted her inexperience. The whole point of sleeping with him was a form of exorcism to free herself from the hold that Dimitris had over her. She just needed to get on with it, Savannah told herself as she kissed him feverishly, pressing her pelvis closer to the tantalising length of his manhood.

'You *are* eager,' he drawled. 'And so am I. You are very beautiful, Savannah.'

He traced his hands over her trembling body and stroked his fingertips up and down her spine, soothing her as if she were a restless colt and he was her master. Savannah's limbs felt heavy as she gradually relaxed. Her cheek was resting on Dimitris's chest, and the powerful beat of his heart made her feel safe in his arms while the storm raged.

This was wrong. Dimitris shoved away the thought that it felt incredibly right for Savannah to be in his bed. The glow from the lamps gave her skin a pearlescent sheen. Her hair was a cloud of spun gold on the pillow and her mouth was lush and tempting. He cupped her breast and felt the hard point of her nipple jutting beneath her bra. Desire kicked hard in his gut, and his erection pressed painfully against the zip on his trousers.

His conscience insisted that he should not have brought her to his room. He should have been stronger and resisted the urgent drumbeat of desire pounding in his veins. He couldn't remember the last time he had been so turned on by a woman that his self-control was threatened. It had been the same ten years ago, a voice in his head taunted him. On the night of Savannah's eighteenth birthday he'd been blown away by her transformation from a shy waitress to a beautiful, sexy woman.

The image she had projected that night had been an illusion, Dimitris brooded. Beneath her seductive party dress she'd been innocent and unworldly, and when he'd made love to her he had been grimly aware that she deserved a better man than him. He hadn't told her that he'd been to blame for his parents' deaths and Eleni's injuries. Selfishly, he had enjoyed Savannah's adoration, even though he'd known that the future she'd hoped for with him would never happen.

But she was different now, he assured himself. Older and more experienced. *Theós*, she had propositioned him and suggested they have sex with no strings attached. Unfinished business. He'd agreed because she had been in his mind for a decade, and he wanted to move on. The chemistry between them had always been white-hot and even though he'd been furious when he'd found her at a hotel with his sister's fiancé, his body had responded on a primitive level, and he'd felt a searing attraction to Savannah.

Why not take what she was offering? He wasn't a hormone-fuelled twenty-two-year-old. He'd had countless lovers and never lost control with any of the women he'd taken to bed. It would be no different with Savannah, he assured himself.

# CHAPTER SIX

SAVANNAH OPENED HER eyes and saw herself. Her reflection in the mirror above the bed was shadowy in the pearly half-light created by moonbeams slanting through a chink in the closed curtains. Dimitris was lying on his stomach beside her. She could not see his face, and his dark head was pillowed on his forearms. Her eyes followed the long line of his spine down to the waistband of his grey sweatpants that sat low on his hips.

He was on top of the sheet, and when she peeped beneath it she discovered that she was still wearing her bra and knickers. Memories of the previous night returned, and she was mortified that *nothing* had happened. She must be the only woman in the world to proposition a man and fall asleep in his bed before the action had started. She'd achieved nothing except to make a fool of herself—again.

Shuffling up the bed, she leaned across to the bedside table and saw the illuminated numbers on the digital clock—two a.m. A touch as light as gossamer brushed across her shoulder. Her heart was in her throat when she turned her head and met Dimitris's unfathomable gaze.

'Did we…?' She needed to check.

He shifted onto his side and propped himself on his elbow. 'If you believe that I'm the kind of man who would take advantage of a young woman who had drunk more wine than was wise, why did you offer yourself to me?'

His voice was controlled, but Savannah realised he was very angry. 'I don't believe you took advantage of me,' she assured him quickly. She hadn't seen him for a decade, but people did not change fundamentally, and she had always felt safe with him.

'I'm glad to hear it.' His eyes narrowed, hiding his thoughts. 'If we had made love you would not need to ask.'

His arrogance should have appalled her but she envied his self-confidence, while hers had taken another battering. 'Wine tends to make me feel sleepy,' she admitted ruefully. 'But I wasn't drunk when I asked to spend the night with you. I knew what I was saying. I appreciate you might have been trying to spare me embarrassment with the excuse that I'd had too much alcohol. But making an idiot of myself is something I do really well, and it's fine to admit that you don't want to have sex with me.'

Dimitris moved so fast that before Savannah could blink she was lying flat on her back and he was on top of her. 'Does this feel like I don't want you?' he growled. The weight of his body pressed her into the mattress and the heat of his skin scorched her.

She caught her breath as she felt the hard length of his erection beneath his sweatpants. With slow deliberation he circled his hips against her pelvis, making her aware of just how aroused he was. The heat of her feminine arousal pooled between her thighs.

'I needed to be sure that you are sure,' he told her. 'If you have changed your mind…?'

She licked her dry lips and saw his gaze focus intently on her mouth. 'I haven't.'

'Good.' The satisfaction in Dimitris's voice sent a quiver of response through Savannah. He moved so that he was lying on his side next to her and skimmed his hand over her body, creating a path of fire from her collarbone down to her hips and back again. He paused to investigate the dip of her navel before moving up to her breast. Savannah sucked in a breath as he stroked his thumb across her nipple. It instantly puckered and jutted against the fine lace of her bra cup.

'You were always *so* responsive,' he growled.

Sensation arrowed down to her feminine core, and she could not restrain a gasp of pleasure when he put his mouth over her nipple and sucked hard. She needed more and groaned her approval when he peeled the damp scrap of lace away from her breast.

The air felt cool on her exposed nipple. He bent his head once again and she speared her fingers in his hair to hold him to his task of licking one taut peak and then its twin. Desire flooded through her, and she was molten between her legs and ready for his exploratory fingers when he moved his hand down and eased the panel of her panties aside.

Savannah was certain that Dimitris held the key to her freedom. She'd held back from making love with other men, even with Hugo during their brief engagement, because on a subconscious level she'd felt that her body belonged to Dimitris. After tonight she would be able to relegate him to the past and in the future she hoped to have new relationships where she could explore her sensuality and perhaps meet a man who would fall in love with her.

At least that was the plan. But when Dimitris brushed his thumb over her moist opening and gently parted her before easing a finger inside her, she was instantly lost to his magician's touch. He muttered something in Greek as he tugged her knickers off and spread her legs wider apart.

When he pushed his finger deeper, gently stretching her, she arched her hips towards his hand, desperate for more of the exquisite sensations he was arousing with his intimate caresses. She gave a little sob of disappointment when he withdrew his finger and rolled away from her.

'Patience,' he murmured in a hoarse tone that sent a shiver of anticipation through her. He had stripped off his sweatpants and the sight of his muscular, hugely aroused naked body made her feel hesitant for a few seconds, especially when she watched him roll a condom down his swollen length.

He positioned himself above her, supporting his upper body with his hands on either side of her head so that he wasn't quite touching her. She melted in the heat of him, and her feminine instincts took over so that she slid her arms around his back and urged him down onto her. The press of his manhood against her opening almost sent her over the edge, but it also felt like the first time, ten years ago, when she had been nervous and unsure.

Dimitris tensed. 'Do you want to stop?'

'No.' She couldn't stop now that she'd got this far. She wanted to spend tonight with him so that she could bury the past. Beneath Dimitris's passionate caresses she recognised that he was holding back from her, as he had done when they were younger. For him it had only been about sex. She understood that now, and she needed to prove to herself that she could sleep with him without her emotions being involved.

He covered her mouth with his and the kiss exploded between them, wild and urgent. Dimitris pushed his tongue between her lips as if he wanted to learn the taste of her again, or as if he'd never forgotten. While their mouths clung, he eased forwards and entered her slowly, filling her inch by inch and waiting while her internal muscles relaxed to accommodate his powerful erection.

It was mind-blowing. A million times better than she remembered, and with a flash of despair Savannah wondered if her outrageous plan had backfired. How could sex with anyone else be better than this?

It got worse, by which her dazed brain meant it got a whole lot better when Dimitris started to move. He rocked forwards and drew back, once, twice, setting a steady rhythm. She lifted her hips to meet each thrust, remembering the synchronised dance they had performed countless times during the eleven nights they'd spent together so long ago. It was as if nothing had changed and now, as then, they moved together in perfect harmony.

He was a fool. But Dimitris could not think about his failings while he was buried deep inside Savannah. He refused to listen to his brain when it pointed out that it had been a mistake to have sex with her—not when it felt so right. More disturbing was the possessiveness that pounded in his blood while he drove into her and took them both inexorably closer to the edge. *She is mine...she is mine.*

The mingled scent of the perfume Savannah wore and her musky feminine fragrance heightened his desire, and he did not care that he'd vowed never to own or be owned by anyone.

One night, no strings. And afterwards he would be free from his memories, and the dreams he sometimes had that she was in bed beside him, but when he rolled over to pull her close she wasn't there and he felt an emptiness inside him—as if everything he'd achieved, his successful career and the money and fame, meant nothing.

One night, already half gone, to sate himself on Savannah's gorgeous body. He'd never expected to meet her again, let alone reacquaint himself with her silken skin and delicate curves. When he'd pushed his shaft into her, she had been so tight that he had almost lost control there and then. He wondered how many lovers she'd had in the past ten years. His instinct told him not many, and there was no reason why that should have pleased him.

Dimitris concentrated on giving Savannah pleasure. Her breasts were especially sensitive, and he loved the moans she made when he used his mouth on her nipples, licking and sucking the swollen peaks while she dug her nails into his shoulders. He slipped his hand between their joined bodies and discovered the hidden nub of her clitoris. She tensed as he rubbed his thumb across her feminine heart while he continued to thrust into her with long, deep strokes.

With a sense of shock he realised that he was about to come, and he gritted his teeth, desperate to hold back the tidal wave. It *never* happened to him. He enjoyed sex but he was always in control. He stilled, and made himself wait, dragging oxygen into his lungs as he stared down at Savannah.

She was so beautiful, her face flushed with passion and her lips reddened from his kisses. Her eyelashes lifted and her eyes were more green than hazel as she stared back at him in a silent communication that went beyond words. Something moved inside Dimitris then, and an emotion he dared not define squeezed his heart.

'Please,' she whispered, locking her legs around his hips as if she feared he would leave her.

'I will please you, *mátia mou*,' he rasped. It was a promise rather than a boast. He pulled back almost completely and gave a powerful thrust, claiming her utterly. She sobbed his name and tremors tore through her as she climaxed hard. Her internal muscles convulsed around him, velvet on steel, and it was too much. The wave crashed over him in an unstoppable, uncontrollable tsunami before throwing him onto the shore, and he was dazed to realise he had survived the storm. But as his heart-rate gradually slowed, his cool logic returned. Sex with Savannah had been amazing, but he hoped she understood that he could not offer her more than physical satisfaction.

Savannah's face was buried in the pillow and she was lying on her stomach. As she came fully awake, memories of the previous night made her feel hot all over. Dimitris had made love to her three times and the night had been a blur of incredible pleasure.

She turned her head cautiously, afraid to meet his too-knowing gaze. To her relief, he was sprawled on his back, his eyes were closed and the steady rise and fall of his chest indicated that he was deeply asleep. Thank goodness for small mercies. Sex with Dimitris had been amazing, beyond compare, although she did not have any other experiences to compare it with.

Still, it had just been sex. Emotion had played no part in their night of passion, she reminded herself. Even when they had lain in a tangle of limbs, breathless, their hearts racing after another shattering orgasm, she must have imagined a connection between them that had felt deeper than their physical compatibility.

At eighteen she had believed that Dimitris's devastating charm and flashes of tender affection were signs that he loved her. But she had witnessed his charisma when he hosted his cooking shows on TV or appeared on chat shows. He was charm personified, the handsome, sexy, hot chef. No wonder women fell in love with him in droves. No wonder she had been besotted with him as an impressionable girl.

It would be easy to fall in love with him again. She longed to waken him with a kiss and arouse his body with her hands and mouth until he took charge and rolled her beneath him or lifted her on top of him and the magic started all over again. But the deal she had made with him and herself had been for one night only. Now it was morning and the cage door was open, ready for her to fly.

Trying to ignore the hollow feeling in the pit of her stomach, she slid carefully across the bed, hoping he wouldn't stir, secretly praying that he would. She located her knickers but couldn't find her bra. The shirt Dimitris had worn at dinner was on the floor and was still damp from the rain, but it was better than nothing, and she slipped her arms through the sleeves.

The problem of getting herself home without her clothes or transport was resolved when she crept out of the bedroom and found her laundered trousers and tee shirt neatly folded on a chair on the landing. Her trainers were there with her handbag and laptop. She dressed quickly, and when she ran down the stairs she met the housekeeper's husband John in the entrance hall.

'I thought I'd try your car again this morning and, to my surprise, the engine started,' he said, handing her the key. 'It could be an intermittent fault with the ignition. I suggest you drive straight to a garage and have a mechanic check the car over.'

'Thanks, I'll do that.'

But as Savannah drove away from River Retreat she knew she couldn't afford to spend money on her car while her finances were in a precarious state. At least she would be paid by Philpot's for the photoshoot, but her conscience pricked that she should buy Dimitris a new phone to replace his that she'd ruined. She had the unsettling thought that he'd taken his revenge by giving her more pleasure last night than she'd known it was possible for her body to experience.

With a murmured excuse Dimitris moved away from the group of party guests he had been chatting to. It was not the first social occasion in the past six weeks where he'd struggled to make small talk, and his jaw ached from forcing a smile. The death of his grandmother a month ago partly explained his dark mood, but his grief for *Γιαγιά* Hestia, who had been nearly ninety after all, was not the only reason for his restlessness.

He walked over to the wall of windows that ran the length of the hospitality suite at Philpot's headquarters in central London. The views from the twenty-second floor were spectacular, especially at night when the illuminated city was spread out in front of him. But he barely noticed the blaze of twinkling lights and turned his gaze towards the door once more, hoping that Savannah would appear. Philpot's PR executive Tara Brown had told him that Savannah had accepted an invitation to the evening's event to mark Dimitris's appointment as the supermarket chain's brand ambassador, and publication of the magazine featuring his recipes and her photographs.

When he'd woken the morning after the incredible night he had spent with Savannah, he'd told himself he was relieved that she had gone. But over the past weeks he'd found himself thinking about her too often for his liking. He could have contacted her through the photographic agency, but he'd resisted. What would be the point? He would not risk having an affair with her. She had meant something to him ten years ago, but he'd hurt her. That was what he did. He damaged the people he cared about. *Theós*, his sister had spent years in a wheelchair because of him.

Dimitris scowled at his reflection in the glass. He'd flown to Rhodes the day after Savannah had left him in Richmond and had spent much of his time testing recipes for his new cookbook. But for once he'd been uninspired by his work, and he had not found solace in the peaceful solitude of his villa overlooking the turquoise Aegean Sea.

He glanced towards the door again, and his heart slammed into his ribs when Savannah walked into the room. She looked stunning in a black velvet cocktail dress that moulded her slender figure and those pert breasts that he had discovered fitted perfectly in his palms. Her hair was caught up in an elegant chignon, and he longed to remove the pins and thread his fingers through the blonde strands.

She gave no indication that she'd noticed him and smiled at a guy who Dimitris recognised had been a lighting technician on the photoshoot at the Richmond studio. He told himself that he was relieved there would not be an awkward situation following their night of no-strings sex. Savannah had evidently moved on, and so had he.

Some forty minutes later his patience had expired after he'd watched Savannah flirt with the men who crowded around her. She laughed often, causing heads to turn in her direction. It struck Dimitris that there was something different about her. A self-confidence she had not possessed at eighteen or even six weeks ago.

He strode towards her with a purposefulness that made her bevy of admirers move away. To his annoyance, his heart was pounding when he stood in

front of her. 'You were so late to arrive this evening that I thought you were not coming to the party.' He managed to sound casual but inside he was fighting an urge to sweep her into his arms and carry her off, caveman style, to somewhere where they could be alone.

Her hazel-green eyes widened, and Dimitris felt a surge of satisfaction that she could not hide her reaction to him. 'I'm surprised you noticed me. You've been knee-deep in attractive women for most of the evening.' Her tart voice only made him want her more.

'You were attracting a lot of male attention.' He was appalled that he sounded jealous. It was an unfamiliar emotion.

Savannah gave him an enigmatic smile worthy of the Mona Lisa. 'I'm enjoying my freedom. I was late because my car broke down and I had to make the rest of the journey by bus.'

'I'll drive you home.'

'It's okay, Alex has already offered to give me a lift.'

'If Alex is the guy who has been trailing after you like a puppy dog, he has been drinking and is probably over the limit to get behind the wheel of a car.'

Savannah's eyes flashed. 'Alex doesn't act like a puppy.'

'Don't tell me he's your boyfriend.'

'I'm not telling you anything. It's no business of yours who I date.'

'*Theós!* Are you sleeping with him?'

'No.' The angry flush on her face made her even lovelier. 'You are the only man I've been to bed with, if you must know.'

He stared at her. 'Since we last slept together a few weeks ago, you mean?'

'I mean ever.' She spun away from him, but he was not going to let her go after that startling piece of information. It seemed impossible, yet he believed her. He felt a stab of guilt when he remembered her faint hesitancy before he'd taken her to bed. Slipping his hand beneath her elbow, he steered her out of the room.

'How is it that I am your only lover?' Dimitris demanded, wondering why he felt so good about it. Possessiveness was another alien emotion to him. 'You are a beautiful, independent woman and you caught the attention of every man at the party.'

'I told you why. I couldn't forget you. But now...'

'Now?' His tone was as dangerous as he felt.

'Now I'm finally free to have other relationships, other lovers. The night we spent together gave me a sense of perspective. The sex was great. Clearly I'm no expert, but I'm sure you will tell me that it wasn't out of the ordinary.'

'That's where you're wrong.' It had been the most

amazing night of his life, but he wasn't about to admit it. 'We are highly sexually compatible.'

She shrugged. 'You must have slept with hundreds of women, thousands.'

'The tabloids are not a reliable source of information.'

Savannah pulled away from him and started to walk quickly along the corridor. 'I don't want this, Dimitris. I don't want you.'

'Liar.' He fell into step beside her as she pulled her phone out of her handbag.

'I'm calling a taxi.'

'I told you I'll take you home.' The lift doors opened, and he followed her into the small space. She glared at him but must have realised that arguing was pointless. Minutes later they walked across the underground car park, and he opened the passenger door of his sleek black saloon. Savannah climbed into the car and her dress rode up, giving him a glimpse of her toned thigh. Desire shot through him, and he silently acknowledged that one night with her had not been enough to satisfy his hunger.

They were both silent on the journey across the city. Dimitris had deliberately not been back to the north London borough he'd left ten years ago, and he was surprised by how little had changed. The high street where his grandfather's restaurant had stood was as run-down as when he had grown up in the area known for its high crime rate. But only a few miles from Camden they drove through picturesque and affluent Hampstead Village, and further out towards the heath the houses were big and gracious with expensive cars on the driveways.

At first glance Pond House looked no different than he remembered. But the shrubs in the front garden were overgrown, the once shiny black gates had rusted and there was an air of decay about the place. He parked on the driveway and switched off the engine.

He felt dangerously on edge and agonisingly aware of Savannah in the close confines of the car. Her perfume teased his senses, and he wanted to press his mouth against the pale column of her neck and feel the erratic thud of her pulse.

'My grandmother died recently,' he said gruffly.

'I'm so sorry.' Her voice was soft with sympathy. 'I remember Hestia when I worked at the restaurant. She was tiny and fierce and kept the waitresses in order, but she was kind too, and devoted to your grandfather.'

Dimitris's throat felt constricted. 'My grandparents were amazing. They still worked in their eighties.' It had been his fault that his grandparents couldn't retire. 'My grandmother passed away peacefully in her sleep. I think she was glad to be reunited with my grandfather.' He drummed his fingers on the steering wheel, wondering what had made him open up to Savannah.

'Would you like to come in for coffee?'

'Sure.'

'The house has been sold,' Savannah explained as she opened the front door. Packing boxes were piled up in the hallway. 'Luckily the new owners are keeping a lot of the furniture, but there's still a ton of stuff to sort out.'

'Have you found somewhere for you and your mother to live?'

She looked away from him, but not before Dimitris glimpsed a sheen in her eyes. Something tugged in his chest. 'Mum has decided that due to her disabilities she needs to move permanently into a nursing home that can provide the support she needs. I've found a wonderful place in Windsor, near to where Mum's sister lives. She is going to move in next week. The nursing home is expensive, but I've calculated that there should be enough money left after paying my father's debts to cover the fees for a while. I'll have to earn a decent income as a freelance photographer so that I can continue to pay for Mum to live at Willow Grange.'

'What about you? Where will you live?'

'I don't know. My studio is at the top of the house, and I'll miss the space and light in the attic room. Finding a new place where I can work is my priority. Various friends have said I can sleep on their sofa.'

Dimitris turned his head when a door opened and a woman in a wheelchair appeared. Illness and worry had aged Savannah's mother and she looked frail.

'Mum, I thought you had gone to bed.' Savannah leaned down to kiss her mother. 'I had trouble with my car and Dimitris drove me home.' She looked at him. 'This is my mother, Evelyn.'

Dimitris stepped forwards. 'I'm pleased to meet you. When my family lived in London my sister went to some of your art classes at the rehabilitation unit.'

'I remember Eleni, of course. And I hear that you are an acclaimed chef now, Dimitris. Your parents would be proud of you.' Evelyn smiled gently. 'The accident when they lost their lives was a terrible tragedy.'

'Yes,' he said brusquely. It would never have happened if he hadn't behaved like a brat.

A woman who was evidently Evelyn's nurse came and helped her into another room. Savannah led the way to the kitchen and filled the kettle. 'There's only instant coffee. I can't afford to buy the proper stuff.'

'Instant is fine.' Dimitris prowled around the kitchen, unnerved by the grief that had hit him hard when Savannah's mother had spoken of his parents.

He pictured his mother's proud smile when he'd grown so tall that he'd towered over her the last summer they had been a family. He remembered watching his father making *tsoureki*, a traditional Greek bread eaten at Easter. The dough was divided into three pieces and shaped into a braid to symbolise the Holy Trinity.

*'The secret is to keep the braid tight to stop the dough expanding sideways while it bakes,'* his father had told him.

Dimitris always remembered that golden rule when he made *tsoureki* every Easter.

His memories shifted to ten years ago, when he had been here at Pond House with Savannah while her parents were delayed abroad. Every evening, after the restaurant had closed, he'd ridden his motorbike at breakneck speed to be with her. For eleven nights they had slept together in her bed and made love endlessly. He'd cooked meals for them in this kitchen, and he had felt closer to her than to any other woman before or since.

But he had known it couldn't last. Nothing good ever did. Her parents had returned, and the same night her father had been waiting for him in the alley behind the restaurant when Dimitris had taken the rubbish out. It had been a fitting setting for the filthy deal he'd been forced to make with Richard O'Neal, he brooded. Richard had bluntly told him that his plans for Savannah did not include her getting involved with a nobody with nothing who was going nowhere. Dimitris had never forgotten Richard's opinion of him, and he'd been spurred to prove the other man wrong.

Ultimately, Savannah and her mother were victims of Richard's criminality as much as the people and organisations he had defrauded. Savannah had admitted that she was practically penniless and soon to be homeless. She was desperate to help her mother, just as Dimitris had been desperate to help his grandparents return to Greece.

There was no reason for him to get involved with Savannah's problems, he reminded himself. The disturbing effect she had on him was a very good reason to walk away. But he did not want to abandon her again. He'd felt bad that he'd hurt her even though he'd acted with the best intentions. He could never come to terms with his guilt about his parents, but at least he could help Savannah and her mother.

'I have a proposition I want to discuss with you,' he said abruptly.

'What kind of proposition?' She looked at him warily and his conscience pricked that the way he'd treated her years ago had made her untrusting.

'I need a photographer to work on my next cookery book. I'm offering you a job, Savannah.'

# CHAPTER SEVEN

'NO. I MEAN, thanks for the offer. It would be a great opportunity, but…' Savannah flushed when Dimitris gave her an enigmatic look.

'But what? You told me that you are trying to build your reputation as a food photographer. Working on my book will give you valuable exposure.'

It was true. Dimitris's cookery books sold millions of copies. He was one of the most successful non-fiction authors in England and North America and it would be a huge boost to her career to work with him. Common sense said she should accept his job offer, but her instinct for self-preservation warned Savannah of the potential pitfalls.

When she'd left him asleep six weeks ago and driven home she'd felt confident that she'd got him out of her system. Dimitris was a skilful lover and he'd taken her body to heights of pleasure she'd never experienced before. But it had just been great sex without emotional involvement.

Since then she had been busy sorting out her father's affairs and organising a nursing home for her mum, and she'd barely given Dimitris a thought during the days at least. Annoyingly, he had invaded her dreams every night. But this evening when she'd spotted him at the party her pulse had accelerated, and she'd avoided him while she'd sought to regain the composure that Dimitris had the power to destroy with one of his sexy smiles. She was dismayed by the effect he had on her and couldn't risk working with him while she was still in the process of relegating him to her past.

'Why do you need a photographer? I know that the acclaimed food photographer Ian Clarke took the photos for your previous books.' Savannah always looked on the back page of cookery books to see who had taken the pictures of the food.

'Ian retired after the last book we worked on together. My publisher agreed that I can choose a photographer who I believe will best showcase my food. Your photos are fun and a little bit quirky, like my recipes. When we worked together on the Philpot's shoot you seemed to instinctively know what I was trying to achieve.'

Dimitris drank his coffee and grimaced. 'I can promise you decent coffee. But seriously, you'll be paid an upfront amount for the commission, and a percentage of the royalties when the cookery book goes on sale. I'm planning a big book with over two hundred recipes and photographs. I've scheduled six weeks to capture all the images, and you will stay at my villa in Rhodes for the duration of the shoot.'

Savannah knew it was unusual for a food photographer to receive royalties. Her potential future earnings would be huge, and she would not have to worry about finding the fees for her mum's nursing home. Dimitris was offering her the chance of a lifetime, but she hesitated.

'I assumed the shoot would be at your studio in Richmond.'

'I like the photos to be taken in natural light, but the daylight will fade earlier in England as the days shorten in the autumn. The clarity of light in Rhodes will give the effect I want of lazy summer days and relaxed living. After all, the title for the cookery book is *A Mediterranean Love Affair with Dimitris*.' He looked amused by her startled expression.

Savannah bit her lip. 'I can't leave Mum and go to Greece.'

'I can wait for a week while you help your mother move into the nursing home. This is a business proposition, Savannah. Nothing more,' he said, as if he wanted to make it clear that he wasn't interested in her for any other reason.

Perhaps working with him and staying at his home in Rhodes would allow her to see the real Dimitris instead of the man of her girlish fantasies or his public image as a sex idol, Savannah thought. She would prove to herself that she was over him.

'I admit I have a personal reason for asking you to work with me.'

Her heart missed a beat at *personal.*

'I would like to help your mother,' Dimitris continued. 'Evelyn was an art therapist at the rehabilitation centre where my sister spent a considerable amount of time when she was a child, recovering from her injures after the car accident.' His voice revealed no emotion, but Savannah sensed that he found it difficult to talk about the life-altering injuries Eleni had sustained in the crash that had killed their parents.

'When I was friends with Eleni at school she told me that she had done some art classes with Mum.'

'Art therapy really helped Eleni to deal with her emotions. She had been a happy, sporty kid, but after the accident she was unable to walk, and she lost interest in everything. Evelyn was wonderful with her, and it is no exaggeration to say that your mother helped my sister to be happy again. Eleni developed her artistic talent and she went on to study jewellery design, and now makes bespoke jewellery for her clients.'

Dimitris looked intently at Savannah. 'I would offer to pay your mother's nursing home fees, but I have a feeling that you won't accept.'

'Mum is my responsibility.' Savannah did not want to be beholden to anyone, least of all Dimitris.

'In that case, I suggest you meet me in Rhodes next week with your camera.'

The following week Savannah fastened her seat-belt when the plane's warning light above her head flashed on. Through the window she could see the spearhead shape of the island of Rhodes, surrounded by a turquoise sea. The guidebook said that Rhodes was the largest of the Dodecanese islands. As the plane began its descent the land below was a chequerboard of green and brown fields, and the towns had white cube houses. The ruins of several ancient landmarks were visible from the air.

Savannah gripped the armrests as the airport runway came into view, not because she was a nervous flier, but the doubts that had tormented her since the plane had left London felt as though butterflies had been set loose in her stomach. She had made the right decision to accept Dimitris's job offer, she tried to reassure herself. It had been difficult leaving her mum, but Evelyn was settling into Willow Grange nursing home and was benefiting from using the hydrotherapy pool. Savannah's priority was to earn enough money so that her mum could continue to receive the care she needed.

After the plane had landed and she'd collected her suitcase and cleared Customs, she walked into the arrivals hall. Dimitris had told her that someone would meet her, and she'd assumed he would send one of his staff. She hadn't expected to see him striding across the concourse.

Her stomach swooped as she stared at Dimitris. She wasn't alone in noticing him. Women of all ages turned their heads to watch him. He looked breathtaking, casually dressed in sun-bleached jeans and a navy-blue polo shirt. His designer shades were pushed onto his head, and he exuded a raw sex appeal that sent a coil of heat through Savannah.

*Breathe*, she ordered herself as she walked towards him.

'Savannah.' His deep voice with a husky accent sent a prickle of awareness through her. 'How was your flight?'

'Fine. Well…there was a two-hour delay. I'm sorry if you have been waiting at the airport for me.'

'I checked the flight details and saw that yours was delayed. You should have accepted my offer to charter a private jet for you.'

She bit her lip, unwilling to explain to Dimitris that she did not want anything from him other than the money she would earn from the photoshoot. They would have a professional working relationship for the next six weeks.

They exited the airport building and he led her over to a sleek red Ferrari. 'My new baby,' he told her as he opened the passenger door. 'Isn't she a beauty?'

'Beautiful, but not very practical,' she noted a few minutes later, after he had abandoned trying to fit her luggage in the small boot of the car and wedged her suitcase and camera bag onto the back seat.

'Maybe not. But she's the love of my life.' Dimitris's grin made him seem boyish and reminded her of the young man she'd been besotted with years ago. He was even more gorgeous now, Savannah thought ruefully, conscious that her pulse was racing. 'When I grew up in a rough London neighbourhood, all the kids dreamed of owning a car like this one,' he told her. 'I was determined to turn the dream into reality.'

Away from the busy roads around the airport the highway hugged the coast, and the views of golden sand beaches were spectacular. Dimitris put the electric sunroof down. The azure sky was cloudless, and the sea shimmered in the bright sunshine. Savannah gave a deep sigh.

'That's how I feel every time I return to Rhodes,' he murmured. 'I can breathe here. I imagine the past week was tough when you moved out of Pond House and took your mother to Windsor.'

'Yes.' Her voice was thick as emotions she had been suppressing for days caught in Savannah's throat. Pond House had been her childhood home, but she had mixed feelings about it since she'd learned that her father had bought the house with money from his criminal activities. She had looked up to her father and respected him for being a brilliant businessman. She'd trusted him even though she'd felt confused and hurt that he did not care about her. Now she was wary of trusting anyone. Her goal was to build her career so that she was financially independent and not reliant on anyone.

This was a new chapter in her life, but Savannah was aware that her mum's life might end prematurely because of her illness. She wiped away a tear and stiffened when Dimitris took his hand off the steering wheel and reached across to squeeze her fingers.

'Witnessing someone you love suffer is the hardest thing,' he said gruffly. Savannah guessed he was thinking of his sister.

'Thank you for arranging a private ambulance to take Mum to the nursing home.'

'Does your mother talk much about your father?'

'Mum has hardly mentioned him since he died. It was a shock at his trial to learn about my father's illegal business dealings.' She turned her head to stare out of the window. 'On the surface we were a happy family, but there were tensions, and however hard I tried at school I felt I was a disappointment to him.'

Dimitris frowned. 'Did you ever discuss your relationship with your father with your mother?'

'Mum was a dreamer, and wrapped up in her art. She made excuses for my father and said he worked hard to provide a good life for us. I had the best of everything, but I felt that I should be grateful to him. I was envious of my friends who had a close relationship with their fathers.'

Dimitris cleared his throat and seemed to be about to say something, but he gave a slight shake of his head and lapsed into a brooding silence for the rest of the journey.

His villa was a vast white-walled property standing in sprawling grounds on a clifftop with incredible views across the bay. Bougainvillea vines smothered with vivid pink flowers grew against the walls, and rosemary and jasmine planted in pots by the front door filled the air with their fragrance. He carried her suitcase and ushered her into the cool and airy entrance hall.

'Welcome to my home, Savannah.'

Home. A lump formed in Savannah's throat at the thought that she was currently homeless. She hadn't had time to look for a flat before she'd come to Rhodes, but she knew that rental properties around Windsor where she could be close to her mum were expensive. Staying with Dimitris for six weeks would give her a chance to look online for somewhere to live when she returned to England.

She did not understand why she'd told him about her difficult relationship with her father that she'd never spoken about to anyone else. From now on she would stick to the boundaries of their working relationship, she decided. She turned and found him standing beside her. The citrus and spice scent of his aftershave evoked an ache deep in her pelvis. Her gaze collided with his and her heart missed a beat when she saw desire glitter in his eyes. With a gasp she stepped away from him as a man walked across the hall towards them.

'This is my assistant, Stefanos,' Dimitris said coolly. His chiselled features were unreadable, and Savannah wondered if she had imagined those few seconds of sizzling sexual awareness between them. 'Stefanos will give you a tour of the villa and bring your luggage up to your room. Meet me downstairs when you are ready.'

The villa's décor was crisply stylish and everywhere was white with touches of grey. The few elegant sculptures and abstract artwork on the walls had probably been chosen by an interior designer. There was nothing to give a clue to the personality of the villa's owner.

The guest bedroom was charming, although Savannah thought that some colourful cushions would break up all the white. She gave a cry of delight when she stepped onto the balcony overlooking the garden and saw an infinity pool that appeared to flow over the cliff edge and into the sea. It had been raining when she'd left London, but in Rhodes in late September the temperature was still as hot as a midsummer's day in England. She thanked Stefanos for carrying her luggage to her room, and when he'd gone she unpacked and swapped her jeans and sweatshirt for a sleeveless linen dress.

Glancing out of the window, she saw Dimitris in the garden with a woman. His arm was draped around her shoulders, and their body language seemed to suggest they shared a close bond. Savannah could not see the woman's face, but she had long, curly dark hair and an enviably curvaceous figure.

Was the exotic brunette Dimitris's mistress? Jealousy burned like acid in her stomach. How could she bear to work with Dimitris every day, knowing that he spent his nights with his mistress? But she had no option. He had handed her a lifeline when he'd offered her the photo assignment and she was determined to ignore her attraction to him.

'Ah, Savannah, there you are,' he said when she walked across the garden a few minutes later. Her brittle smile turned to shock and delight when she recognised his attractive companion.

'Eleni?'

'Savannah, it's so good to see you. Dimitris told me that you are the photographer for his new book.' Eleni's vivacious face was even prettier than when she had been a teenager. She walked a little stiffly over to Savannah and flung her arms around her. 'You haven't changed a bit.'

'But you don't use a wheelchair.' Savannah hugged her school friend. 'I didn't recognise you.'

'I'm able to walk thanks to my brilliant surgeon in America.' Eleni sighed. 'It's bad timing that I'm flying to the Far East tomorrow to attend a series of jewellery fairs. But we have this evening to catch up on ten years of news.'

'I'll leave you girls to chat,' Dimitris said. 'We'll eat outside on the terrace in half an hour.'

Savannah waited until he'd strolled back to the villa and took a deep breath. 'Eleni, there is something I need to tell you. I went on a couple of dates with Matt Collier after he told me he was single. I had no idea he was engaged to you until Dimitris found us at a hotel. Please believe that nothing happened between me and Matt.'

'Dimitris explained the situation when he told me that you would be working with him on his book,' Eleni said ruefully. 'I still feel hurt and angry with Matt for lying to me. He lied to you too. I know you wouldn't have dated him if you had known he was engaged. We were best friends at school, Savannah, and I've never forgotten your kindness when I was bullied by some of the other girls.'

'Dimitris was furious.'

'My brother has always been very protective of

me. Sometimes a bit too protective.' Eleni sighed. 'Dimitris seems to blame himself for the car accident when our parents were killed and I was badly injured.'

'How could it have been his fault?'

'I don't know. I think I told you before that I have no memory of what happened. I wish I could persuade Dimitris to talk about the crash. It must have been traumatic for him and I'm sure it's not good for him to bottle things up. He has been amazing in the way he has taken care of me, and he paid for the surgery that enabled me to walk again.'

Eleni led Savannah over to a terrace where a dining table stood beneath a pergola covered with vine leaves and bunches of plump red grapes. 'Tell me about yourself. You were engaged, weren't you? I remember that Dimitris was in a bad mood for days when he heard the news.' Eleni did not hide her curiosity. 'I knew that the two of you were dating when we lived in London. Dimitris won a lot of money with a lottery ticket and days later he took me and our grandparents to Rhodes, where he'd bought a house for us. The move was so sudden, and I wondered if something had happened between you and him to cause you to break up.'

Dimitris was not likely to have told his sister that he'd been able to afford to buy a house in Rhodes with money he'd accepted as a bribe from her father, Savannah thought grimly. A winning lottery ticket had been a perfect excuse. Her anger ignited when she remembered how miserable she'd been after he had abruptly ended their relationship. At eighteen she had been starved of affection from her father, and she'd wanted to believe that Dimitris loved her. She wondered now if he had shown an interest in her because her family had been wealthy.

She had been fixated with Dimitris, and she was dismayed that he could still affect her. When they had arrived at his villa and she'd sensed the chemistry between them, she'd acknowledged that sleeping with him hadn't got him out of her system as she'd hoped. But she knew that Dimitris would never love her the way she yearned to be loved—totally and unconditionally. She'd spent her childhood trying to win her father's love, and she was not going to waste any more of her emotions on Dimitris.

Perhaps she would sign up to a dating app that some of her friends used, and when she returned to London after the photoshoot she intended to socialise more. She couldn't let her bad experience with Matt Collier put her off. But, deep down, Savannah wondered if she was unlovable, and it was the reason her father and Dimitris had rejected her.

A sound from behind her alerted her to Dimitris's presence, and her treacherous body reacted instantly as each of her nerve-endings zinged and her nipples hardened so that her lacy bra scraped against the sensitive peaks. She fought the urge to cross her arms over her chest as her gaze was drawn to his face and she recognised the flare of desire in his dark blue eyes before he looked away from her.

It was a relief when Eleni's cheerful voice broke the tense silence. 'What are we having to eat? Mmm, *pastitsio*,' she said when Dimitris placed the serving platter he was holding on the table and removed the lid. 'It's the Greek version of lasagne,' she told Savannah.

'I know that *pastitsio* is your favourite dinner, *paidí mou*.' Dimitris spoke to his sister in an indulgent tone that Savannah had never heard him use before. Something twisted inside her that she was ashamed to admit was envy. Dimitris loved his sister and he had loved his grandparents. After he'd dumped her, she had told herself that he was heartless, but now she had evidence that it wasn't true. He just hadn't loved her.

Once again Savannah's feeling of insecurity, that stemmed from her father's indifference, surfaced. When she was a model, men had admired her for the way she looked. Ten years ago Dimitris had wanted to have sex with her, but he had trampled on her girlish dreams of romance and happy ever after. Now she was going to spend the next six weeks working with him and living in his home, but she would be on her guard against his potent charm.

* * *

Dimitris opened the bifold doors of his kitchen studio and took a deep breath of sea air. He loved the villa, and his favourite place was the studio that stood apart from the main house. Below the cliff was a secret beach, accessible by a set of steep steps carved into the rocks.

The studio was not just his workplace where he developed recipes and ran his business empire, it was his sanctuary. The views of the bay and the crystal-clear sea were stunning. His own piece of paradise. Not bad for a boy who had grown up in a rough part of London and failed most of his exams at school because he'd been too busy helping to run the restaurant and taking care of his grandparents and orphaned sister to have time to study.

He had money, two beautiful homes and a flashy car—all the trappings of success, but there was an emptiness inside him that material possessions could not fill, and guilt was a dark shadow over him. He'd distracted himself with sexual liaisons with women who understood that he wasn't in the market for a relationship. But since he'd slept with Savannah two months ago he'd felt restless. On the few occasions recently when he'd invited a woman to dinner his libido had taken a hike and at the end of the evening he'd driven them home rather than ask them to spend the night with him.

Things had been worse since Savannah had

come to stay at the villa. His awareness of her was a constant throb in his groin and he felt like a teenager fired up with hormones. He told himself it was a normal response to a beautiful, sexy woman. In other circumstances Dimitris would have pursued his sexual interest and instigated an affair. But he held back from Savannah for the same reason that he had fought his growing feelings for her years ago.

For eleven magical nights her sweetly passionate response to him had aroused his body and touched his soul. She had made him forget what he had done, and that he did not deserve her love. But when Savannah's father had more or less forced him into a despicable deal, Dimitris had accepted money from Richard O'Neal because he felt responsible for his grandparents and sister. He acknowledged that it had given him an excuse to break up with Savannah before his fledgling feelings for her had deepened.

Dimitris raked his hand through his hair. Usually he was relaxed while he was working on a new book, but he felt edgy and unsettled. For the past two weeks he had spent hours every day with Savannah while she photographed each stage of the recipes he prepared. He hadn't employed a food stylist or art director because he liked to keep things simple he'd explained on the first day of the shoot, when she'd asked about other members of the art team.

While Savannah was taking photos she often had to lean across him for a close-up shot of a dish, and Dimitris knew from the giveaway pulse thudding crazily at the base of her throat and the swift rise and fall of her breasts that she was aware of the sexual energy between them, and trying to ignore it, as much as he was.

There was a month remaining of the schedule to complete the cookery book and he hoped his self-control would last. It had to because he could not risk sleeping with her. He knew she was attracted to him, but he sensed that she would hope for more than sex if they had an affair. But sex was all he wanted. Physical satisfaction without commitment. He had hurt too many people in the past, including Savannah, and he didn't want anything else on his conscience. Knowing that he had caused his parents' deaths would haunt him for ever.

His nostrils flared as he watched her slide off the stool where she had been sitting at the counter and working on her laptop. Like him, she was wearing denim shorts. Hers were cut high up on her thighs, and her long legs had acquired a golden tan from the warm Greek sun. Her vest top moulded her breasts, and it was obvious that she wasn't wearing a bra.

Desire kicked in his gut as he imagined slipping his hands beneath her top and fondling her breasts. He watched them bounce when she walked towards him, and his jaw clenched. Her hair was caught in a high ponytail with blonde tendrils framing her face. She looked at once wholesome and sexy and she was sending him out of his mind.

'I'm ready when you are,' she said, hooking her camera bag over her shoulder. 'I'll admit that when you suggested cooking and photographing the seafood recipes down on the beach, I thought you were mad. But I've been looking at the mood board we created before we started shooting. All the other shots have been taken in the studio and although we have used different props it will be good to do something different.'

He nodded. 'It would be easy to take a picture of the sea or the beach and use it as a backdrop, but I want readers to almost smell the salty air and feel the sea breeze when they look at a photo of absolutely fresh prawns cooked with ouzo and a rich tomato sauce.'

Savannah grinned, and for once her diffidence with him slipped. 'You're making me feel hungry.'

*You are having the same effect on me.*

Dimitris gave a silent groan and turned away to pick up his backpack, which held the ingredients he would need plus cooking pans and a portable stove for outdoor cooking.

'The beach looks an awfully long way down,' she said minutes later when she stood beside him on the top of the cliff and looked over the edge.

'I'll go first. The steps are steep but take it slowly

and you'll be fine.' Dimitris had climbed the steps hundreds of times. He paused halfway down and glanced over his shoulder at Savannah. She was pale and looked terrified.

'I'm not great with heights,' she admitted.

'*Theós*, why didn't you say so?'

'You planned to do the shoot on the beach, and it's my job as a professional to take the photographs that you want.'

He swore. 'Turn round and climb back up the steps. We'll think of another idea.'

'No.' She took a deep breath. 'I'm all right. Let's keep climbing down.'

Dimitris did not know whether to admire her determination or feel frustrated by her stubbornness. He walked up the steps to where she had frozen and held out his hand. 'Hold onto me and we'll go down together. I won't let you fall.'

She took his hand without hesitation, and he felt a mix of emotions at her trust in him. Would she have such blind faith if she knew that his stupid behaviour had been the reason his parents had died? He was at a loss to understand the urge that had come over him to tell Savannah about the accident. He had never admitted to anyone that he had been responsible, not even Eleni—especially Eleni. His sister's childhood and teenage years had been ruined and he was to blame. All he could do was ensure that Eleni's life was as good as he could make it.

While his mind was in the past, Dimitris had made a slow descent of the steps and guided Savannah down. She let out a shaky breath when they reached the bottom. Some colour had returned to her cheeks, but he couldn't forget how scared she had been.

'What a beautiful, secluded beach. It was worth the climb.' She kicked off her trainers and ran into the sea to paddle. 'The water is so warm. I wish I'd brought my swimsuit. Is it safe to swim here?'

'Yes, there aren't any strong currents.'

Dimitris set up the portable stove on some flat rocks and walked over to where Savannah had sat down on the sand. She was staring pensively at the waves that rippled against the shore. 'Why are you afraid of heights?' he asked, dropping down beside her.

'It's silly. An irrational fear from something that happened when I was younger.'

Dimitris thought of how his stomach cramped whenever he was driving and saw a lorry travelling in the opposite direction. He had to steel himself not to hit the brakes and trust that the lorry wouldn't collide with his car. 'Events in childhood can affect us when we are adults,' he said gruffly.

Savannah sighed. 'It was nothing really. I fell off my horse when I was thirteen. I wasn't a very confident rider, but my father insisted that I learned to ride because he said it was what posh people did. He spent a fortune on a thoroughbred horse, but Merlin was too big and strong, and I couldn't control him. I was competing in a gymkhana in front of a big crowd when my horse refused to jump over a fence. I was petrified,' she admitted. 'Merlin stopped dead and I was thrown over his head. I remember being in the air and looking down at the ground, knowing it was going to hurt when I landed.'

'Were you injured?'

'Not seriously, luckily. I was bruised and shaken. While I was lying on the ground and crying, my father stormed over and yelled at me for being stupid. He was furious that I'd made a fool of myself and him.' Savannah bit her lip. 'My father always made me feel that I was a disappointment to him. Needless to say, I never rode a horse again. When I was standing at the top of the cliff, I imagined myself falling.'

'I would not have suggested doing the photoshoot on the beach if I'd known about your fear of heights.' Dimitris frowned. 'When we knew each other before, I had the impression that you and Richard were close. You often spoke about how wonderful he was, and I believed you were a daddy's girl.'

'I pretended that he was the kind and loving father I wished he was. I think I hoped that if I imagined hard enough it would be true.' Savannah sent

Dimitris a wry glance. 'I was good at make-believe. I fooled myself that you were in love with me because I was looking for affection that I didn't get from my father.'

Dimitris cursed silently. Richard O'Neal had told him a shocking secret, but it was not up to him to explain the truth to Savannah. Only her mother could do that, and perhaps Evelyn had her reasons for withholding information that Savannah had a right to be told.

'Now Richard is dead you might find it easier to talk to your mother about how you felt that he hadn't been a loving father,' he suggested.

Savannah shrugged. 'There's not much point now. Mum is struggling to come to terms with the fact that my father was a criminal.'

Dimitris stood up and offered his hand to help her to her feet. Savannah's issues were not his business, he reminded himself. After the photoshoot she would return to her life in England, and they were unlikely to meet again. It was odd how his heart sank at the thought.

When Savannah put her fingers in his, he remembered how she had trusted him when they'd climbed down the cliff steps. She rose gracefully to stand beside him, and he tensed when he breathed in the seductive scent of her perfume. Her eyes widened and were more green than hazel. Dimitris was certain she felt the prickling awareness in the atmosphere between them. His heart was thudding, and he could not make himself move away from her. She was so beautiful. His brain told him to resist the hunger that heated his blood, but his gaze was riveted on her mouth as he lowered his head towards her.

One kiss. That was all he wanted. *Liar*, he mocked himself. He was desperate to pull her down onto the sand, remove her clothes and his, and make love to her. *Desperate* suggested a lack of control that Dimitris would not tolerate. He jerked away from Savannah, breathing hard. Her parted lips were a temptation he must resist. Colour spread over her face at his rejection, and he felt bad. But she'd just told him that she had yearned for affection from her father. Her vulnerability now made her off-limits.

'We should get on with the photoshoot while the daylight is still good,' he said, already striding up the beach.

The cookery book would give Savannah an income in royalties that would allow her to pay her mother's nursing home fees. Years ago, Evelyn had helped his sister and it was for that reason he'd asked Savannah to photograph his recipes, Dimitris reminded himself.

He cursed when he searched in the backpack and discovered he'd left a bottle of olive oil behind in the kitchen studio. 'I'll have to go back for the cooking oil while you start setting up your camera,' he told her.

But when he climbed the steps to the top of the cliff and looked down at the beach he saw that Savannah had taken advantage of his absence to pull off her shorts. She tugged her top over her head, baring her breasts. Dimitris's mouth ran dry as he watched her wade into the sea wearing just her knickers. *Theós!* She would tempt a saint, let alone someone as flawed and guilt-ridden as him. He did not deserve her, and Savannah deserved a much better man than him.

# CHAPTER EIGHT

'MY NEW RESTAURANT in Crete opens tomorrow night. I'd like you to come to the launch party with me.'

Savannah looked up from her laptop screen as Dimitris strolled into the small sitting room off the villa's open-plan living area that she used for an office. Working in the evenings gave her an excuse to avoid him, which was vital after he had nearly kissed her on the beach a week ago.

Her face burned as she remembered how he'd stopped when his lips had been centimetres above hers. It was not the first time Dimitris had rejected her, but it would be the last, she vowed. Hence after they ate dinner together at the end of a long day working in the kitchen studio she always headed straight to her office. It was unfortunate that the window overlooked the pool where he swam most evenings. The sight of him wearing black swim briefs that left little to her imagination evoked an ache of longing low in her pelvis.

Dimitris had made it plain that he wasn't interested in her, and never again would she offer herself to him as she had done at his house in Richmond, she promised herself. Her plan to get him out of her system hadn't worked, Savannah acknowledged ruefully. But they were halfway through the photo-shoot, and outside of working hours she just had to avoid him as much as possible for the next three weeks. That would be difficult if she accompanied him to a party.

'Surely you have a PR photographer to take pictures at the launch party.' Savannah turned her attention back to her screen. Dimitris looked gorgeous in jeans and a loose cream shirt with the top buttons undone, giving her a glimpse of his tanned skin and wiry black chest hairs. She prayed he couldn't see the betraying hard points of her nipples beneath her thin cotton dress.

'My public relations team will take promotional photos at the restaurant. I intend to use the event to promote my new cookery book and I'll give a couple of interviews to the media. I need you there to talk about how you photographed the recipes.'

He crossed the room noiselessly and Savannah snatched a breath when he spun her chair round so she was facing him. 'There's no need for you to work editing photos until late every evening,' he said with a frown. 'The schedule for the book is on track. The launch party of Hestia's Crete will be a good opportunity to raise your profile as a food photographer. The restaurant is the tenth in the Hestia's chain since I opened my first restaurant here in Rhodes.'

'Did you use the money you accepted from my father to fund your business?' She could not hide her bitterness. It was important to remember that Dimitris had broken her heart once before. Savannah sensed it would be easy to fall for his sexy charm again. When they worked together in the studio she'd discovered that he was clever and entertaining, and he had a sharp wit. He made her laugh with stories about the various kitchens he'd worked in when he'd been a junior chef. It was dangerous to like him, Savannah reminded herself.

'No,' Dimitris said heavily. 'I spent the money from your father on a house for my grandparents and to pay for some of my sister's medical treatment. Everything I have achieved in my career has been the result of the long hours I spent perfecting my cooking. I was lucky to be given some great opportunities and worked hard to get to where I am today.'

Savannah chewed her lower lip. 'I don't have anything to wear to the party.' It was the only excuse she could think of.

'Leave it to me. I'll organise a dress to be delivered to the villa tomorrow.'

'I don't…' She broke off when Dimitris gave her an impatient look.

'I expect you to accompany me to the party. It's not negotiable. Promoting the book is part of your job,' he said coolly before he strode over to the door. Savannah succumbed to the childish urge to stick her tongue out at his back as he left the room.

The next day, after working in the studio, Savannah went to her room and found a large flat box on the bed. Inside was a dress that she knew must have cost much more than she could afford. Hopefully, her credit card would take the strain. The money she'd earned from the Philpot's shoot had nearly all gone on her mum's nursing home fees.

She showered and blow-dried her hair before catching it in a loose chignon. The dress was a full-length silk sheath in olive-green with a low-cut bodice and narrow shoulder straps that meant she couldn't wear a bra. The dress fitted like a dream, and she had to admit that the colour and the simplicity of the style suited her slim figure. Another box contained a pair of silver stiletto heel sandals and a matching purse.

Would Dimitris think she looked good in the dress he had chosen for her? She wished she didn't care about his opinion, but her heart was thumping when she went to meet him.

He walked across the entrance hall while she was halfway down the stairs. When he saw her, his jaw firmed as an almost feral expression pulled his skin tightly over his hard cheekbones.

'You look stunning.' The flare of desire in his eyes lit a flame inside Savannah. But she was confused. After he hadn't kissed her on the beach she'd assumed that he'd suppressed any attraction he might have felt for her.

Dimitris looked breathtaking in a black tuxedo. His hair was more groomed than usual, although it still curled at his nape, and the dark stubble on his jaw was neatly trimmed. When Savannah reached the bottom of the stairs and walked towards him, the spicy scent of his cologne evoked a tug of longing in the pit of her stomach.

'Come into the sitting room. I have something for you.' He ushered her into the room and handed her a slim velvet box. Inside was an exquisite peridot pendant on a gold chain and a pair of peridot and diamond earrings. Savannah closed the lid and gave a tiny sigh of regret as she held out the box to him.

'The jewellery is beautiful, but I can't afford it. The dress probably cost the earth.'

'I don't expect you to pay for the dress or the necklace,' Dimitris said coolly. 'I asked you to attend the party with me and I have simply provided you with an outfit to wear.'

Savannah bit her lip. The dress was one thing but… 'I can't accept the jewellery,' she insisted.

'Most of the women on the exclusive guest list at the launch party will be showing off their diamonds.' Dimitris opened the box and lifted the pendant from its velvet cushion. He moved behind Savannah and fastened the gold chain around her neck. She could not disguise a shiver of reaction when his fingers brushed across her skin. 'Wear the jewellery tonight, hmm?' he murmured. 'It's not a big deal, but if you want to you can return it to me after the party.'

She could hardly refuse. Savannah stepped in front of the mirror and fixed the earrings to her lobes. The peridot pendant nestled in the hollow between her breasts and when she turned around Dimitris's gaze lingered on the low-cut neckline of her dress. He moved away to collect her camera bag from the coffee table where she'd left it, and she released her breath. The simmering sexual attraction between her and Dimitris threatened her already shaky composure.

He had chartered a helicopter to fly them to Crete, the largest of the Greek islands and hugely popular with tourists. His new restaurant was located next to a pretty harbour full of fishing boats. When they arrived, the sun was a fireball sinking into the sea and staining the sky pink and gold. A steady stream of guests arrived in cars, boats and helicopters which landed on the helipad on the roof of the restaurant.

Dimitris had said the guest list was exclusive and Savannah recognised several international celebrities. During her short modelling career she'd attended many glamorous events, but nothing as grand as this. The paparazzi had gathered outside the front of the restaurant to snap pictures of the guests, who posed by the door before they stepped inside to enjoy a champagne reception.

She stiffened when Dimitris placed his hand on her waist to guide her to where they were to stand for the publicity shots. Intense media coverage of the opening night of the restaurant was important to attract customers to Hestia's Crete. Dimitris was the star of the evening, and he was relaxed and smiling and drop-dead sexy in front of the cameras.

'Smile,' he instructed as she stood tensely beside him. 'And try to relax. We have been working hard recently, and it's time to have some fun.'

Savannah's heart gave a jolt in response to the gleam in Dimitris's eyes. She was determined to ignore her fierce awareness of him when he kept his hand on her waist as they entered the restaurant. After he'd greeted his guests he led her over to a few journalists, who asked questions about the new cookery book and Savannah's role as the photographer. She coloured when Dimitris described her as one of the best food photographers in the business.

'Let me show you the kitchen,' he said, catching hold of her hand as he opened a door at the rear of the restaurant.

Unsurprisingly, the state-of-the-art kitchen was bustling and chaotic. The staff were clearly excited to see him. The head chef Kostas spoke English and explained to Savannah that several of the young chefs had received financial support during their training from Dimitris's charity which helped youths from underprivileged backgrounds.

It was obvious that Dimitris was revered by the staff, and he spoke to each of them, asked about the food they were preparing and joked with them while Savannah unpacked her camera and took photos of the dishes for the promotional campaign.

'All the youngsters want to be a famous chef like Dimitris,' Kostas told her. 'They are inspired by him. He devised the recipes on the menu when he came and spent days here in the kitchen. He asked for their ideas and suggestions and encouraged them. Dimitris is their hero. He made it to the top, but he never forgets that he started at the bottom.'

During the five-course dinner, which was superb, Savannah's thoughts returned to the past. She had been devastated when her father told her that Dimitris had accepted a bribe to dump her. 'I set your boyfriend a test,' Richard O'Neal had told her.

'If he genuinely had feelings for you he would have refused the money. But he took it, and it proves that he felt nothing for you.'

Dimitris had used the money to help his elderly grandparents to retire and he'd paid for his sister's medical care for the injuries she had received in a car accident that Eleni had suggested he somehow blamed himself for. He had worked hard to become successful. Unlike Savannah's father, who had made money from crime and who had left her mum destitute. She sighed. It would be so much easier if she could label Dimitris a villain and hate him for hurting her feelings when she'd been eighteen. But he was a complex man, and the truth was she had been searching for love that her father had withheld from her.

'Do you not like the food?' Dimitris murmured when Savannah toyed with her dessert. *Kataifi* was made with chopped walnuts and flavoured with cinnamon, wrapped in a crispy, buttery dough and drenched in a lemon-scented syrup.

'It's delicious, but I've eaten too much,' she said ruefully. 'I'll have to do some exercise to work off the pounds I'm sure to have gained.'

'You could swim in the pool instead of watching me from your office,' he said drily.

She gave him a startled look, mortified that he might think she had spied on him in the pool.

He quirked one eyebrow. 'I wondered if you were avoiding me.'

'We work together in the studio every day,' she muttered.

'But you prefer not to spend time with me after work?'

Savannah's temper flared as she wondered where he was going with the conversation. What did he want from her? 'I had the impression on the beach a week ago that you want us to be work colleagues and nothing more.'

His dark blue eyes were unfathomable, but she noticed a nerve flicker in his cheek. He sipped his wine before he said softly, 'Is that what you want, Savannah?'

She was about to assure him that of course it was. Anything other than a strictly work based relationship with Dimitris would be dangerous. But she was transfixed by his masculine beauty, and when he smiled she felt more alive than she'd done in ten years. 'I don't know,' she admitted huskily.

The band had been playing smooth jazz tunes during dinner, but now the guests had finished eating and the tempo of the music increased as people stepped onto the dance floor.

Dimitris pushed back his chair and stood up. He offered his hand to Savannah. 'Would you like to dance?'

Not a good idea, her brain cautioned. But if she

refused it might arouse his suspicion that she was fighting her attraction to him. Taking a deep breath, she placed her fingers in his. He led her to the dance floor and placed his hands on her waist as they moved to the beat of the music. The brush of his thigh against hers made her insides melt. Savannah had only drunk one glass of champagne, but she felt intoxicated by the heat of his body and his male scent: spice, pheromones—desire.

It was nearly midnight when the last guests left the restaurant. Dimitris called all the front of house and kitchen staff together and thanked them for their hard work making the opening night a success.

'The head chef told me that a percentage of the profits from your restaurants is paid to your charity and funds a training scheme to teach young people how to cook,' Savannah said after they had climbed into the helicopter, and it took off.

Dimitris nodded. 'I was lucky that my grandfather taught me how to cook, and I was able to develop my skills at catering college. Many kids are not given the chance to start a career, especially when Greece experienced economic problems in the past years. I'm glad to put something back into the industry that has enabled me to be successful.'

'You must feel proud of everything you've achieved.'

'Must I?' His voice was strangely grim, and he looked away from Savannah and stared out of his window. She didn't understand the reason for his change of mood. At the restaurant he had been charming and when they had danced together he'd flirted with her, and it had taken all her willpower not to fall under his spell.

They were both silent for the rest of the flight to Rhodes. Savannah had never flown in a helicopter at night. It was magical sitting in the cabin and looking out at the dark sky scattered with stars that seemed close enough to touch.

When the villa came into view she sensed that some of Dimitris's tension had eased. The helicopter landed and he jumped out and offered his hand to help her down the steps. They walked past the infinity pool that looked pretty, lit with multicoloured underwater lights. The water flowing over the edge disappeared into the darkness.

Savannah's pulse thudded as a memory of Dimitris standing at the edge of the pool before he dived in came into her mind. She pictured his broad, tanned chest covered with dark hairs that arrowed over his flat abdomen and disappeared beneath the waistband of his swim briefs, and heat coiled through her.

'How about that swim for the exercise you said you needed?' He grinned at her startled expression, and she felt herself blush as she wondered if he had somehow guessed that she'd had erotic thoughts about him.

'It's late and I think we should go straight to bed.' Horrified that he might think she had propositioned him, she said frantically, 'I mean alone, to our own beds, obviously.'

Dimitris halted and turned her towards him, cupping her chin between his fingers to tilt her face up to his. 'I think that might be what is known as a Freudian slip,' he murmured, amusement and something else in his eyes that sent a quiver of excitement through Savannah. He rubbed his thumb absently over her jaw and the unexpected tenderness in his caress chipped at her fragile defences.

'I want to make love to you, Savannah. And I think you want me too.' Beneath his almost casual tone was a rough note of sexual hunger that evoked a moist heat between her legs. But this man had wrecked her emotions when she had been young and vulnerable, and even though she was older and, hopefully, wiser she was afraid to give in to the desire running rampant through her body.

He lifted his other hand and ran his finger from the base of her throat, down her décolletage to the hollow between her breasts, where the peridot pendant gleamed in the moonlight. It was impossible to hide from him the jerky rise and fall of her chest as she fought the temptation to sink against his whipcord body. He captured her hand and carried it to his mouth to brush his lips over her palm and then the inside of her wrist, where her pulse was going crazy.

His other hand still cupped her jaw. He traced his fingers over her cheek and up to her ear. His touch was as light as gossamer and her resistance melted beneath his sweet seduction when he lowered his head and moved his lips over her cheek. The delicious abrasion of his stubbled jaw on her skin aroused her unbearably and the temptation to tip her head back so that he could claim her mouth with his own was overwhelming. His closeness and the glittering desire in his eyes when he lifted his head and stared down at her made her feel as weak as a kitten.

'One night was not enough for either of us, was it, Savannah?'

Dimitris's voice broke the spell he'd woven around her with his skilful seduction.

'How many nights would be enough?' she asked tautly. 'Five, ten? There are twenty-two nights left until the photoshoot is finished. Will you have tired of me before then?' Savannah pulled away from him, desperate to hide the riot of her emotions.

His eyes narrowed. 'Is it necessary to quantify a time period that our relationship might last? We both want to be lovers, so why not take things one day at a time?'

'Relationship!' She huffed out a breath. 'You have said publicly in the media that a relationship and commitment are not what you want. But they are what I want. At least the possibility of something more meaningful than casual sex.'

Dimitris frowned and Savannah said quickly, 'I don't deny that I am attracted to you. I can't hide the way I react to you. But having sex to scratch an itch is not enough for me.'

*'Theós!'* he exploded. 'In what way have I acted as though I view making love to you as simply a way to satisfy my baser instincts? We have grown close in the past few weeks.'

'So we would be friends with benefits?' She bit her lip. 'Dimitris, you told me that your car is the love of your life. Yes, we have got on well while we've worked together, but you don't allow anyone to get too close, do you? Not emotionally, and certainly not me.'

'Is that what you want?' he gritted. 'For me to lay bare my deepest feelings?'

She gave him a wry look. 'Do you have any deep feelings?'

'How about my guilt, and self-loathing. Are they enough *feelings* for you?' He raked his hand through his hair. His jaw was clenched, and his eyes were almost black with fury and something else. *Pain*, Savannah realised with a jolt of shock.

'Dimitris…you don't have to…' Too late, she realised she had opened Pandora's Box and she was desperate to close it again so that he would not look like he did right now…wrecked. He wasn't made of granite, he was a flesh and blood man, and he was hurting.

'You started this,' he told her harshly. 'You might as well hear all of it.'

'I killed my parents.' Dimitris heard Savannah's swift intake of breath and reminded himself that he deserved the look of shock and horror that flared in her hazel-green eyes. 'Not directly,' he said grimly, 'but I caused the accident in which they died, and my sister was so badly injured that it seemed impossible she would walk again.'

*Do you have any deep feelings?*

Savannah's question had opened the floodgates and he could not hold back the tidal wave of self-recrimination from pouring out. He had more emotions than he could handle, and a long time ago he'd stopped trying and had locked his feelings away in a box labelled *Do Not Open.*

He had meaningless affairs with women who were too self-absorbed to wonder who he was beneath his public façade of a careless playboy. He was aware that his success was in part due to his sex appeal. Women wanted the Hot Chef, the Greek god in the kitchen, and no one had ever tried to discover the man he really was—except for Savannah.

She was looking at him with a mixture of curiosity and concern in those incredible eyes of hers.

'How could you have caused the accident? You were what? Fourteen or fifteen? You can't have been driving the car.'

Memories—*pain*—surged through him. 'My parents were taking Eleni to her ballet class,' he said heavily. 'I was supposed to have ridden my bike to football training, but I'd overslept and persuaded my mother to drop me at the sports centre.'

If only he'd woken earlier, his parents would not have died. The seeds of the accident had been sown when he'd forgotten to set his alarm. Dimitris could never forgive himself for his stupid mistake that had such tragic consequences.

'My mother was driving.' His voice rasped in a throat that felt like he'd swallowed broken glass. There was almost a sense of relief in opening up to Savannah, even though he was sure she would despise him once she knew the truth. He'd spent almost two decades fooling other people, fooling himself that he was fine. But he wasn't fine, and he was fairly certain that Savannah saw through him.

'I'd got in with a bad crowd at school, but that's no excuse. I was a brat.' His jaw clenched. 'An argument started about my attitude. I was unkind to my sister and Eleni started crying. My father turned around and told me to apologise, but I was rude to him. My mother took her eyes off the road and looked over her shoulder at me, in the back of the car.'

Dimitris tasted bile in his throat as he relived the moments before the crash. 'For those few seconds while my mother's attention was distracted, the car veered out of the lane. A lorry was travelling in the opposite direction. In the split second when I realised we were going to hit the lorry, I shouted a warning. I think my father grabbed the steering wheel. But it was too late, and it was a head-on collision.'

'Oh, God. It must have been horrific.' Savannah's voice was gentle. Dimitris did not understand why she hadn't recoiled from him in disgust. 'But you were not responsible for what happened.'

'Of course I was responsible,' he said savagely. 'I've explained how I had distracted my mother.'

The police had taken a statement from him as part of their investigation into the cause of the crash, and he'd told them that his mother had momentarily lost concentration. He'd later heard that the lorry driver had survived. For months afterwards Dimitris had expected to be arrested for causing the crash. But just because no one else blamed him did not mean that he was blameless. He knew what he had done, and now Savannah knew.

'The last words my mother spoke to me were that my family were concerned about me…and they loved me.'

'Oh, Dimitris. It was an accident. It wasn't your fault.' Savannah's eyes were fiercely bright, and tears clung to her lashes. With a jolt of shock he realised that she felt sympathy—for him.

'Don't you dare suggest that I wasn't to blame,' he said savagely. He *knew* it was his fault, and he couldn't understand why Savannah was not convinced of his guilt. 'Eleni spent years confined to a wheelchair because of my stupidity. How do you think she'd react if I told her how the accident happened?'

'I think you should talk to her about the crash. She told me she has tried to discuss it, but you clam up.'

'If I admitted to my sister what I had done she would have every right to hate me.' He turned away from Savannah while he struggled to bring himself under control. There was a hollowness in his chest as if his heart had been ripped out. *This* was why he avoided emotions. It was easier not to care about anything.

'Eleni was all I had left of my family. Of course I had my grandparents, but they were heartbroken to lose their only son and their grief added to my guilt. I couldn't bear that Eleni would blame me because she was an orphan and couldn't walk. I vowed to take care of her and work hard to provide for her and give her the best life I could.'

Savannah came to stand in front of him. 'I'm certain that Eleni wouldn't blame you. She adores you, and she would want you to stop blaming yourself.'

He shook his head. He'd carried his guilt for so long and despite what Savannah had said he knew there could be no absolution for him. He was furious with her for suggesting there could be. She put her hand on his arm and he flinched even as his damnable desire for her sparked into flame. His emotions—*Theós!* he hated that word—felt raw, and he couldn't handle the understanding in her eyes, he couldn't handle *her* when he felt a stupid urge to cry like a child.

'I need a drink.' He shrugged off her hand and strode towards the poolside bar. Her heels clipped against the tiled floor as she followed him, and he cursed and swung round to face her. 'Go to bed, Savannah.'

His control felt dangerously close to snapping. He wanted to take her right there on the tiled floor, shove her dress up to her waist and free his aching erection from his trousers to sink into her slick heat. He longed to make love to her until there was nothing in his head but her softness and heat and the scent of her perfume that he did not doubt would haunt him for as long as he lived.

'Go!' he bit out. 'You were right, I can't give you what you want.' He didn't wait for her to respond, and when he walked away and she did not follow he told himself he was glad.

# CHAPTER NINE

SAVANNAH STOOD BY her bedroom window and watched Dimitris in the pool. He swam length after length without pausing, as if he wanted to push himself to his limits, or as if he was punishing himself. She sensed it was the latter.

It was her fault. Guilt was an arrow through her heart. His pain and his need to keep on swimming, up and down, up and down, was his way of dealing with his agonising emotions after she'd accused him of not having deep feelings. How wrong she had been. And how cruel. Because her instincts had told her that the real Dimitris was a far more complex man than the charming, sexy chef he presented to the world.

The truth was utterly heartbreaking. Since he was fourteen—an age when many teenagers were impressionable—he had believed that he was responsible for his parents' deaths and his sister's life-changing injuries. And for eighteen years he had not told anyone of his secret torment, until she'd challenged him to reveal the pain he'd carried inside him for so long.

But it had not brought him comfort to finally speak about the accident. She'd been unable to convince him that he was blameless, and he had rejected her sympathy—rejected her. Tonight he had admitted that he desired her, but she'd acted like the teenage girl of ten years ago who had yearned for a fairy tale. Dimitris was not a fantasy prince, he was a man with flaws, but there was much to admire. His kindness when he'd offered her a job so that she had enough money to take care of her mum, his patience and understanding when she'd told him why she had a fear of heights, and he had shown his philanthropy with his charity that helped train young chefs.

He was a flesh and blood man, and she had made him bleed. Savannah closed her eyes, hating herself for being so blind. Dimitris's self-containment was not because he did not have feelings, it was a defence to hide his guilt and grief.

Where did they go from here? For a start, she could admit that she wanted to make love with him again. She looked back at the pool and caught her breath as Dimitris hauled himself out of the water. Naked, he truly was a Greek god. His toned, tanned body was long and lean, with hard thighs and a broad, muscular chest. He stood under the poolside shower and the spray flattened the whorls of black hairs on his chest. Her gaze followed the arrowing of hairs over his abdomen and down to where they grew thick around the base of his manhood.

Heat unfurled low in her belly, a hunger she could not deny. Life was unpredictable and could be over in an instant in a collision of metal hitting metal. Life could be cruel, as her mum's diagnosis of a degenerative disease had proved. Life was for living *now*, not worrying about what would happen in the future. Dimitris did not want permanency, but she was prepared to accept an affair with him on his terms. After all, he couldn't break her heart if she did not give it to him.

His bedroom was on the same floor as hers, but at the front of the house overlooking the sea. She knew he must still be downstairs, and she did not hesitate before entering his room. The sight of the big bed sent a throb of nervous anticipation through her. Dimitris had given her a glimpse of the man behind the mask, and now it was her turn to let him see how badly she wanted him.

A breeze stirred the filmy curtain in front of the open door leading to the balcony. The sound of waves breaking onto the sand enticed Savannah outside. Twinkling lights lined the bay and the night sky was crowded with glittering stars. Minutes later she heard the click of the bedroom door and took a deep breath before she pushed the curtains aside and stepped into the room.

Dimitris froze and his eyes narrowed on her. He was wearing a towel knotted around his waist, and droplets of water clung to his chest hairs. He threw his clothes onto a chair before he spoke.

'What do you want, Savannah?'

'You.'

His lack of a reaction did not surprise her. No doubt he regretted revealing the emotions that he'd kept hidden for his entire adult life and he'd spent nearly an hour in the pool re-establishing his iron control over himself.

There was only one way to show him that she was serious. She slid the straps of her dress over her shoulders and shimmied out of the clingy sheath, slowly baring her breasts, her midriff and her hips. The green silk slithered to the floor, and she was left in just a black lace thong.

Still Dimitris said nothing, but his chest rose and fell as if it hurt him to breathe when she walked towards him.

'One night was not enough for me either,' she told him. 'I don't care how long we last.' She stretched out her hand and loosened the towel, but when she tried to pull it away he clamped his hand over hers.

'Are you offering pity sex?' he growled. 'For some reason you feel sorry for me and so you've decided to sleep with me?'

She shook her head, feeling her heart shatter a little when she thought of the burden of guilt he'd carried for so long. 'I don't pity you. I want to make love with you,' she said simply. She whipped the towel away and curled her fingers around his powerful erection. 'I'm pretty sure you want me too, but just to be sure…'

Her heart thudded as she sank to her knees in front of him. She had never done this before. But she needed to show him that she was his, utterly, for as long as the fire between them blazed.

'Savannah?' His voice was low and harsh, and he spoke her name like a warning—or a plea—when she ran her tongue over the tip of his manhood.

He muttered something in Greek and speared his fingers in her hair as if he intended to pull her head up and prevent her pleasuring him with her mouth. At least she hoped she was giving him pleasure. She was fascinated by the combination of steel and velvet against her tongue and was fairly sure that his ragged groan was of enjoyment, not because he wanted her to stop.

'What am I going to do with you, *mátia mou*?' The huskiness in Dimitris's voice made Savannah's heart contract.

She sat back on her heels and looked up at him. The hunger in his dark eyes intensified the ache between her legs and moist heat pooled there in readiness for him. How could this be wrong when it felt so gloriously right? She smiled. 'I hope you will think of something,' she said softly.

*Theós!* That smile. Impossibly, when Savannah smiled she was even more beautiful. Dimitris shuddered as she licked her tongue along his hard length. She was sending him out of his mind.

When he had discovered her in his room, his heart had crashed into his ribs. She was a goddess in her green silk dress that moulded every dip and curve of her body. He had told himself that ordering a dress for her to wear to the party was a reasonable thing to do. After all, she would be promoting his new cookery book. He'd bought the jewellery on a whim when he'd seen the gems displayed in a jeweller's window in Rhodes Town. The peridots reminded him of the mysterious green of Savannah's eyes.

But when he'd seen her glide down the stairs before the party, looking so beautiful that he'd felt a tug in his chest and his blood had surged into his groin, he'd realised that he was in trouble. He'd been unable to take his eyes off her all evening, and he had known that Savannah's prickliness had been her attempt to hide her awareness of him.

He did not understand how she could smile at him after what he'd told her. He *had* been responsible for the tragedy that had destroyed his family. His sister had spent years in a wheelchair because he'd been a stroppy, ungrateful teenager who hadn't deserved his parents love and he did not deserve to find love for the rest of his life.

Dimitris tensed. He could not think properly while Savannah was using her mouth on him so effectively that he realised he was seconds away from embarrassing himself and disappointing her. He never lost control. The truth was that no other woman had tested his control the way Savannah did. She made him feel things he was not ready to admit to himself, and so he shoved a lid on his emotions—he was good at that—and drew her to her feet, pulling her close so that her body was plastered against his.

Her stunning eyes, more green than hazel tonight, widened when she felt his erection jab between her thighs. 'I want you,' he told her rawly. He needed to lose himself in her sweetness and forget for a while who he really was, what he had done, and how he could never be good enough for her.

He lifted her into his arms and carried her over to the bed. She was a lightweight, but his heart thudded painfully hard when she looped her arms around his neck so that her breasts pressed against his chest.

'Are you sure this is what you want?' he asked when he laid her on the bed. 'I can't give you…'

She silenced him by pressing her finger gently across his lips. 'All I want is to make love with you.'

He liked the shiver that ran through her when he removed the scrap of black lace from between her legs, and he liked even more the gasp she made when he pushed her thighs apart and lowered his head to lick his tongue over her moist opening. The scent of her feminine arousal made his gut clench and he wanted to simply drive his rock-hard erection into her to find the release he craved.

But this was all about Savannah and he told her so, not in words but with his hands and mouth and tongue as he gave her the most intimate caress of all while she gasped and squirmed and arched her hips towards him.

'Please, Dimitris. I want you *now...*'

He understood that her need was as fierce as his, and neither of them could wait any longer. Pausing to take a condom from the bedside drawer and sheath himself, he moved over her and slid his hands beneath her bottom, tilting her pelvis. And then he entered her with a hard thrust, and she gave a low cry and wrapped her legs around his hips. It was like a homecoming, and he almost came too soon.

He forced himself to take things slower and concentrate on her needs. He kissed her mouth, her throat, and trailed his lips over her breasts that were flushed rose-pink from the heat of her desire. Her nipples were dusky rose and swelled beneath his tongue when he sucked on them, and her guttural moans tested his control. Somehow he hung on and drove into her faster, harder, setting a rhythm that became increasingly urgent.

Savannah bucked beneath him and dug her fingernails into his buttocks. He held her there at the edge as he stared into her eyes, and he felt a connection that stunned him, a tenderness that terrified him. And then she smiled, and something inside him cracked. He felt the first ripples of her orgasm and withdrew a little way before he thrust deep into her molten heat. Her internal muscles tightened around his shaft and with a groan he let go and tumbled with her into the abyss.

Savannah opened her eyes to find the room bathed in the pearly light of dawn. She wasn't in her room. Memories of the previous night flooded her mind, and she turned her head and saw Dimitris, lying beside her. He was asleep and she studied his handsome face. His features were softer, and his long black lashes made crescents on his cheeks. The stubble on his jaw was thicker with a night's growth and his mouth…*his mouth*… Heat coiled through her as she remembered how skilfully he had used his mouth on every inch of her body to give her incredible pleasure.

With a sigh she acknowledged that she had jumped into the fire, but she didn't regret sleeping with him. She knew that great sex was all he would offer, and she accepted it. She hoped that if they were lovers for the few weeks remaining of the photoshoot, their chemistry would fizzle out and she would truly be over him.

Dimitris moved his head on the pillow. He was still asleep, but he made a low groan. He brought his arm across his face. '

*'No...no!'*

He sounded in such terrible torment that Savannah wanted to weep. Another groan was torn from his throat and sweat ran down his face.

*'Are my parents all right? And my sister? Are they alive? No...'*

'Dimitris.' Savannah touched his shoulder. 'Wake up. You were having a dream.'

His chest heaved, and he sat up and stared at her, but it was as though he did not see her. 'Eleni…?'

'It's okay, Dimitris. Let it go.'

He blinked and jerked fully awake. His mouth twisted as he shrugged Savannah's hand off him, and she tried not to feel hurt by his rejection of her sympathy. 'Let it go?' He laughed, a low, raw sound without humour. 'How can I let go of the memories of what I did? It was my fault.'

She realised he was still half trapped in his dream. 'Do you often have nightmares?'

He raked his hair off his brow, and Savannah noticed that his hand shook. 'A few bad dreams are nothing compared to what my sister suffered for years after the accident.'

'Talk to her. Perhaps you will be able to come to terms with the past if you stop holding back from your sister,' Savannah told him gently. 'I had a message from Eleni, saying that her business in Asia will finish next week and she is to return to Rhodes for a few days before flying to America.'

'Eleni's trip to Boston is for her final check-up at the spinal injury hospital.' Dimitris's jaw clenched. 'I know I must explain what happened, but I can't expect her to forgive me any more than I can ever forgive myself.'

He threw back the sheet and stood up. 'I'm sorry I disturbed you, Savannah,' he said tonelessly, in control of his emotions once more. 'It's still early. I suggest you go to your room and get some more sleep.'

Dimitris's heart was hammering, and his mind was full of terrible images of the car—a tangled heap of metal and the front barely visible where it had come to rest beneath the lorry. It was a miracle that he'd been pulled from the wreckage almost unscathed, one of the medics at the scene had said. No one had told him then that his parents had died in the crash. His grandfather had broken the news to him later when his grandparents had returned from the hospital where they had been visiting Eleni in the intensive care unit.

How could he forget? How could he let go of his guilt? He stumbled into his bathroom and locked the door behind him, needing to be alone, yet a part of him longed for the comfort of Savannah's cool hand on his shoulder. He did not deserve her gentle sympathy, he reminded herself as he stood beneath the punishing cold spray that could never wash away his self-loathing.

Eventually he dried himself and walked back into the bedroom. He stopped dead at the sight of Savannah asleep in his bed. The sheet lay across her waist and her bare breasts were perfect creamy mounds tipped with dusky pink nipples. The early morning sunlight, slanting through the blinds, danced over her sexily messy blonde hair and her slender limbs that were tanned a pale honey colour.

She was so beautiful, inside and out. He felt an odd constriction in his chest when he remembered her fierce insistence that he had not been responsible for the accident that had destroyed his family.

The ache in certain areas of his body were a reminder that he had made love to her twice more last night. Both times had been less urgent than the first, but just as intense. When he moved inside her they fitted perfectly together as if they belonged. Fanciful nonsense of course, he assured himself. Good sex—it had been sublime—was still just sex.

Last night had been amazing, but now it was morning and he needed to re-establish boundaries that had been crossed when he'd opened up to Savannah in a way he'd never done with anyone else. There was three weeks remaining of the photoshoot for his cookery book, and immediately afterwards he had a trip arranged to Australia for a promotional tour. Whatever he felt for Savannah would have burned out by then, he assured himself.

He wasn't ready to face her while his emotions still felt raw and exposed, like an onion that had been peeled layer by layer. He left her sleeping and went downstairs to the kitchen. It was his assistant Stefanos's weekend off. Dimitris made a jug of coffee and loaded a tray with a bowl of thick Greek yogurt, honey and some plump figs.

He stepped outside to the garden and picked mint leaves to tear over the figs. God knew why he impulsively cut a long-stemmed pale pink rose and placed it on the tray. When he returned to the bedroom he found Savannah sitting up in bed. She watched him warily as he put the breakfast tray on the bedside table.

'Sorry, I must have fallen back to sleep. Are you…okay?'

'I'm fine.' Confession wasn't good for the soul, whatever anyone said. He regretted that she had seen him when he was weak. It wouldn't happen again.

'I meant to go to my room, but I was tired after…' She broke off and blushed.

Dimitris couldn't remember the last time he'd seen a woman blush. It was a reminder that Savannah was different, more vulnerable, than the lovers he'd had in the past, who'd had no expectations from him.

'I enjoyed last night, and I think you did too,' he drawled. He did not want her to think that taking her to bed had been about anything more than satisfying their mutual desire.

Her breathing quickened when he sat on the edge of the mattress and tugged the sheet away from her breasts. 'We should get up and start work in the studio,' she said huskily.

'Have you forgotten it's the weekend?' He pulled the sheet down, and hunger tore through him as his gaze lingered on the vee of blonde curls between her thighs. He wanted to make love to her and lose himself in the sweet solace of her body, to banish the shadows of his nightmare.

Dimitris stripped off his sweatpants and lay beside Savannah on the bed. His erection nudged between her thighs when he lifted himself over her and supported his weight on his elbows. 'Weekends are when we relax,' he murmured. His nostrils flared as she reached down and curled her fingers around his hard shaft.

'You don't feel very relaxed to me. Quite tense in fact,' she teased him softly.

'Witch.' He didn't know what to make of her. She made him laugh. *Theós*, she had almost made him cry. Savannah made him feel things he was afraid to define, and he told himself it was desire that caused his heart to pound when he entered her with a long, deep thrust and smothered her gasp with his mouth.

The kiss was wild and hot before it became slow and sensual, with an underlying tenderness that only Savannah had discovered lurked in the depths of his soul and which he could not hide from her. He moved inside her, and she matched his rhythm, lifting her hips each time he drove into her with steady strokes, taking them closer to the edge.

It couldn't last, and she gave a sharp cry as she shuddered beneath him, and he felt the exquisite tightening of her internal muscles around his shaft. Moments later he reached his own shattering climax, and afterwards a sweet lassitude swept over him and he rolled onto his back, taking her with him and holding her close.

Much later Dimitris unravelled from Savannah and they balanced the tray on their knees while they feasted on tart yoghurt and juicy figs. She chased a tiny shred of mint leaf across her lips with her tongue and he couldn't resist using his own tongue to lick off a smear of honey from the corner of her mouth.

'Tell me about your father,' he said, propping himself against the headboard. 'It must have been a shock when he was accused of corruption.'

'It felt like a bad dream.' She bit her lip and glanced at him as if she was remembering how she'd woken him from his nightmare. 'Although I didn't have a close relationship with my father I respected him until I discovered that he was corrupt to his core. The stress of his trial accelerated Mum's illness, I'm sure.'

Dimitris searched her face for any sign that she knew the truth about Richard O'Neal. 'Were your parents happily married?'

She frowned. 'I never heard them argue. They had quite separate lives. My father was always working, and Mum was busy with her art. I don't think they were particularly close.'

Savannah hesitated. 'A few years ago I helped Mum sort out some old letters and paperwork she kept in her bureau. Tucked at the back of a drawer was a photo of a young man. She took it from me and got upset when I asked who he was. My father was still alive then. I wondered if she had been in love with the man, but something had happened, and she'd married my father.'

Dimitris slid out of bed and walked outside to his private balcony. Could the man in the photo be

Savannah's real father? he brooded. He felt guilty that he was keeping a shocking secret from Savannah. But he could not reveal what Richard O'Neal had told him. The person who should tell her the truth was Savannah's mother.

'Dimitris?' Savannah's voice was soft with concern, and when she joined him on the balcony the gentle expression in her eyes chipped at the ice around Dimitris's heart. 'I know you are worried about telling Eleni everything you told me. But she has a right to know the details of the accident. And one day you might be able to put the past behind you.'

'Why do you care?' he asked gruffly. 'I hurt you in the past.'

'I wish you had confided in me ten years ago. But I was immature, and I wanted you to rescue me like the handsome prince from the fairy tales I'd read as a child. I wish I had tried to get you to talk about your parents.'

Dimitris felt an ache in his chest when he remembered her at eighteen, so beautiful and trusting. There was a wariness in her now that he guiltily acknowledged he was responsible for. He wished he were different and could give her the fairy tale. But at the end of the photoshoot he would let her go so that she could find her prince. He was stunned by how much he hated the prospect, and how bleak the future seemed without Savannah.

He pulled away from his thoughts and smiled. 'I thought that after breakfast I would take you out on my boat to visit some of the other islands around Rhodes. Symi and Halki are both pretty islands.'

'A boat trip sounds amazing.' She caught her breath when he lifted her up so that her pelvis was flush to his and she felt his burgeoning erection. 'We've eaten breakfast,' she reminded him when he carried her inside and tumbled them onto the bed. 'So are we going on your boat now?'

'I didn't specify how long after breakfast we would go on a boat trip, *mátia mou*.' He grinned as he eased between her splayed thighs so that his swollen tip pressed against her moist opening. 'But I have a feeling it will be *much* later.'

# CHAPTER TEN

DIMITRIS SHOVED HIS hands in his pockets and turned away from the window where he had been staring unseeingly at the beach. His sister looked up from her book. 'I wish you would sit down. You have been prowling around the room ever since I arrived.'

He walked over to Eleni and lowered his tall frame onto the sofa beside her. In his mind he heard Savannah's voice urging him to open up to his sister. 'I need to talk to you…about what happened in the accident.' He pulled in a breath. 'Or rather why it happened.'

'Actually, I know what happened.' Eleni closed her book and gave him her full attention.

He frowned. 'Did you speak to Savannah?'

'Not about the accident. But when I mentioned to her that I wished I knew the details, she suggested that there might be a police file or some documents about the accident. I don't know why I'd never thought of it. I did some research and found an old newspaper report. All I knew was that our car had been in a collision with a lorry. The report said that the lorry had a tyre blowout that caused the driver to swerve across the road and into the path of a car.' She blinked away a tear. 'Our parents were in the front seats and didn't stand a chance.'

'That's not how it was.' Dimitris jumped up and stared at his sister. He had never followed up about the accident or looked for reports because he hated to be reminded of the worst day of his life. Besides, he knew what had happened and the part he'd played. 'I was responsible for the crash. I distracted Mum, who was driving, and she took her eyes off the road. I was a vile teenager and I made you cry. It was my fault that our parents were killed, and you were injured.'

Eleni stood and walked stiffly towards him. 'The newspaper said there was an inquest, and the cause of the crash was recorded as an accident due to a tyre blowout. The lorry had been properly maintained before the crash, and no one was to blame. It was a tragic accident.' She put her hand on his arm. 'Maybe you did do something in the car and Mum was distracted. But you were not responsible for the crash.'

Dimitris shook his head. 'I was to blame.' His mind reran the seconds before the crash, when he'd seen the lorry heading towards the car. He'd believed that his mother had swerved across the road, but the truth was it had happened so quickly, and he couldn't be sure. If the lorry's tyre had burst and the driver had lost control of the vehicle perhaps it had contributed to the chain of events. It did not change things though. 'If I hadn't behaved like a brat, Mum would have been able to focus on driving,' he told his sister. 'You spent years in a wheelchair because of me.'

'I can walk again because of the pioneering surgery you paid for.' Eleni put her arms around him. 'Dimitris, it's time to let go of the past. You don't need to feel guilty, and I certainly don't blame you. The truth is I barely remember our parents, but you have taken care of me and protected me since they died.'

Savannah rolled her shoulders that were aching after she'd spent too long sitting in front of her laptop. Editing photos was just as important as actually taking the shots and allowed her to make fine adjustments to lighting, tint balance and contrast to achieve perfect images.

Dimitris walked into the studio, and she felt a familiar flutter of excitement in her stomach when he stood behind her and slipped his arms around her waist. He looked over her shoulder at the screen. 'These pictures are excellent. It was a good idea of yours to serve the *souvlaki* on a bed of orzo salad. The chicken on skewers looked boring frankly, alone on the plate, but the red tomatoes, black olives mixed with the white orzo in the salad bring the whole dish to life.'

'I'm going to adjust the brightness a fraction more and then I'll be happy with the pictures.' Savannah couldn't hide the little tremor that ran through her when Dimitris nuzzled her neck before sliding his mouth up to the sensitive spot behind her ear.

'You are a perfectionist, and I admire your dedication to your work, *mátia mou*.' To her disappointment he moved away and raked his hand through his hair. 'I spoke to my sister.'

Savannah's eyes widened but she did not say anything as she waited for Dimitris to continue.

'Eleni took your advice and researched information about the accident. Even though it happened eighteen years ago, she found a newspaper report which stated that the cause of the crash was a tyre blowout on the lorry.' He exhaled heavily. 'I still believe that I was partly to blame for distracting my mother. But Eleni doesn't blame me.'

'She loves you very much,' Savannah said softly.

*And so do I.*

The words slipped into her head, and she felt as though her heart was being crushed in a vice. She was in love with Dimitris. In spite of her determination not to fall for him, he had dismantled her barricades one by one. But the way she felt was different to when she had been eighteen.

This overwhelming feeling wasn't a teenage crush, this was the real thing. She hadn't put Dimitris on a pedestal. She knew he wasn't perfect, but she loved the imperfect bits—his grouchiness first thing in the morning before he'd drunk two cups of strong coffee, his obsession with flashy sports cars and his habit of telling her what happened in a film if he'd seen it before, so that she wasn't disappointed with the ending, he said.

She was madly in love with his sexy grin and his way of looking at her when she was talking as if he was utterly fascinated by her. She loved his enthusiasm when he took her sightseeing around Rhodes and other islands nearby. Most of all she loved how he brought her body to life with his clever hands and mouth. When he made love to her and gave her more pleasure than she'd imagined it was possible to experience, she had to remind herself that it was just amazing sex. For Dimitris at least.

It was all he wanted, and he had never pretended otherwise or promised more. There was just over a week left of the photoshoot and then he was due to fly to Australia, and she would return to England and try to get on with her life. Her heart contracted at the prospect of their affair finishing. It was too late to try to protect herself from being hurt, but it was her fault, not his.

She decided to enjoy the short time she had left with him, and every night of the following week she told Dimitris with her body what she dared not reveal to him with words. Her insecurity from growing up believing that her father did not love her meant that she was wary of revealing her emotions in case she was rejected.

For his part Dimitris made love to her with a new urgency and wild abandon, as if he was aware of the days slipping past increasingly fast. The cookery book was ahead of schedule and when it was finished he'd suggested a trip on his boat to the island of Kos at the weekend.

The last chapter was Greek desserts. Savannah had spent all morning trying to achieve the perfect shot of a chocolate mascarpone baklava with coffee syrup, but the layers of filo pastry stacked on top of each other between layers of chocolate mascarpone had kept slipping and the dish looked a mess.

Dimitris had said it was because the coffee syrup was too thin, and he decided to make re-make the dessert from scratch. The atmosphere in the studio was unusually fraught, and Savannah had a new worry that made her tense and on edge. Her period was four days late. It had never happened before, and she was always as regular as clockwork.

It was probably a blip, she reassured herself, but when Dimitris had driven her to Rhodes Town earlier in the day, so she could buy souvenirs for her mum, she'd nipped into a chemist and bought a pregnancy test. She planned to do the test in the morning, but meanwhile she felt slightly sick after eating a large portion of the abandoned baklava and hoped the nauseous feeling was a sign that her period was about to start.

A sudden loud clatter followed by a curse drew Savannah's attention across the studio. Dimitris had dropped a baking tray onto the counter, and the dozen pastry baskets that he'd painstakingly assembled were in pieces. Her handbag that she'd left on the counter had been knocked onto the floor.

'That's why you should always wear an oven glove to take a metal tray out of a hot oven,' he growled. His annoyance quickly faded, and he gave her a rueful grin.

'Did you get burned?'

'It's not too bad. I'll run my hand under the cold tap after I've rescued your bag.' He crouched down to pick up the contents of her bag that were strewn over the floor.'

'I'll do it,' Savannah said quickly. But she was too late. Dimitris straightened up slowly and held out the pregnancy test kit.

'What the hell?' His smile had disappeared, and his eyes were as cold as black ice.

'I'm a few days late.' She bit her lip when he stared at her as if she'd grown a second head. 'It's probably nothing to worry about.'

Or it might be a baby. For the first time Savannah actually allowed herself to think about what that meant. She'd hoped to have a family one day, but she'd assumed she would meet the right man and marry him before children came along. Life rarely went to plan, and she might be pregnant with Dimitris's baby. The idea evoked an unexpected fierce tug of longing in her.

Dimitris was scowling as if an accidental pregnancy was her fault. Her temper flared. It took two people to create a child.

*If there was a baby.*

In an instant she'd gone from it being a possibility to believing it was true—because she would love to have Dimitris's baby. She had been falling in love with him over the weeks they had spent together, working, laughing, making love. But the fantasy she'd built up in her mind that he would come to love her was crumbling before her eyes.

*'Theós!'* He dropped the pregnancy test on the counter as if it had burned him. 'You had better go back to the villa and do the test.' His jaw clenched. 'I'll meet you in a few minutes, and if it's positive we'll have to discuss what to do.'

*Discuss what to do?* Savannah watched Dimitris stride over to the sink and shove his burned hand under the tap. She bit her lip so hard that she tasted blood. If she was pregnant she would have her baby, there was no question in her mind. Dimitris could do what he damned well liked. But his attitude told her that he wouldn't want to be involved with his child. He had looked appalled at the prospect of her having his baby.

With a low cry she ran out of the studio. He expected her to go to the villa to do the test, but she was certain she was pregnant. She had all the symptoms—sensitive breasts, nausea and a missed period. She couldn't face giving Dimitris the proof of her pregnancy that would make him furious. She wanted to be alone, but there was nowhere for her to go except down to the secret beach. Dimitris wouldn't look for her there.

Savannah tried not to look at the sheer drop over the cliff. She had climbed down to the beach with Dimitris a few times, but he always went first and guided her down the steps. Her fear of heights was irrational, and it had started when she was thrown from her horse. She was angry that the incident when she'd been a child still affected her.

She remembered how nervous she had been at the prospect of taking her horse over a set of jumps in the riding ring. But her father had been keen for her to compete, and unusually he had come to watch her. In her imagination she'd pictured herself making a clear round over the jumps and her father proudly applauding when she'd received a rosette. Instead she had lost control of her horse and when she'd been lying on the ground, humiliated and tearful, her father had yelled at her and told her she was a disappointment.

'Savannah, what the hell are you doing?'

She glanced over her shoulder and saw Dimitris at the top of the cliff. Her eyes were blurred with tears, and she missed her footing and found herself falling through the air. It happened so quickly that she didn't have time to scream. She had been two-thirds of the way down the cliff, and she banged against rocks before landing heavily, face down on the sandy beach.

'*Theós!* Savannah…' Dimitris sounded odd. She heard him run down the steps, but she was too winded to speak and tell him she was okay. She was aware that various places on her body hurt, and she kept her eyes closed while she tried to get over the shock of what had just happened.

'Savannah.' Strong arms gently turned her over and she opened her eyes and saw Dimitris's haggard face. He expelled a ragged breath. 'I thought…' He shook his head. 'Never mind what I thought. Are you hurt?'

She moved gingerly. 'My hip hurts. I must have knocked it against the rocks.'

He pushed her skirt up to her waist, and even though she'd bounced down the cliff Savannah felt a familiar curl of heat in her belly when he ran his hands over the tops of her legs. 'You have some nasty grazes on your hip and thigh, and more grazes on your arms and shoulder.'

He lifted her carefully into his arms. His face showed no emotion, but a nerve flickered in his cheek as he carried her up the steps. Dully, she thought that if there had been a baby there might not be one now because of her stupid behaviour.

Dimitris carried her all the way back to the villa and put her in the car. The hospital was a short distance away, and when they arrived he scooped her up and strode into the accident and emergency department.

She was glad that the doctor spoke English. He first checked that she wasn't suffering from concussion. 'Your grazes and bruising are not serious, but the pain in your hip might indicate a fractured bone and it will be necessary for you to have an X-ray.' He wrote a few notes and glanced at Savannah. 'I must ask if there is any possibility that you could be pregnant.'

She dared not look at Dimitris, standing next to her hospital bed. 'Yes.'

'In that case it will be best if you do a pregnancy test before we can continue with an X-ray. The chance of radiation affecting an unborn child is very small, but if you are pregnant there are extra safety measures we can take to minimise the risk.'

* * *

Dimitris stared out of the hospital window. His car was below in the car park, an attention-grabbing scarlet speed machine that was even better than the poster of a sports car he'd stuck on his bedroom wall when he was a boy growing up in a deprived part of London. He'd promised himself that one day he would make his fortune and own the car of his dreams.

He wouldn't be able to cart a baby around in the Ferrari, and the boot was too small to fit a pram in. *Theós!* He forced back a wild laugh. How could there be a baby? He had never considered having a child. A baby would require responsibility, commitment, and love—everything that Dimitris had successfully avoided all his adult life, with the one exception of his sister.

He guessed that the frantic thud of his heart was a sign that he was in shock. When he'd seen Savannah tumble down the cliff he'd experienced the same sickening terror that he'd felt in the car, seconds before it had ploughed headlong into the lorry. When he'd raced down the cliff steps he'd expected to find Savannah's crumpled and lifeless body on the beach, and his relief that her injuries appeared not to be serious had evoked a stinging sensation behind his eyes. He'd suppressed his emotions, something he was so good at, and focused on getting her to the hospital as quickly as possible.

Dimitris pinched the bridge of his nose as the emotions he'd felt on the beach pushed through his defences. When Savannah had told him that she might be pregnant it had felt like a bomb had exploded and his life would never be the same again. He hated the sense of not being in control, and of events happening that frankly scared the hell out of him.

He heard a slight noise behind him and swung round as Savannah walked into the room. His gut clenched at the sight of the large purple bruise on her shoulder and more bruises and grazes on her arms and legs. But it was the wounded expression in her eyes that hurt him the most because he knew he was responsible. To say he had not reacted well to her possible pregnancy would be an understatement.

'What is the result of the test?' he asked tautly.

'I had a blood test because pregnancy in the first weeks can be detected earlier than with a urine sample. We'll know the result in a few minutes.'

'I don't understand how it could have happened. We were always careful.'

'Don't worry, Dimitris. If I am pregnant you won't have to be involved.'

Her scathing tone scraped his raw emotions. 'If you are pregnant I am already involved. I won't shirk my responsibility for the child.'

'For God's sake!' she snapped. 'Your attitude is why I won't want you involved. I don't want my baby to grow up with a father who is only around out of a sense of duty. Children pick these things up. I always felt that my father didn't love me, and I used to think I'd done something wrong.'

Guilt kicked Dimitris in his gut when he thought of the secret that Richard O'Neal had told him. He had to somehow persuade Savannah to talk to her mother about her father.

After what felt like several lifetimes the door opened and the doctor walked into the room. 'The pregnancy test is negative,' he told Savannah. 'So we can proceed with the X-ray of your hip. The nurse will come to take you to the radiology department.'

'Well, that's that,' she muttered after the doctor had gone. 'I'm sure you must be relieved.'

'Aren't you?' In fact Dimitris did not feel elated as he'd expected. But why on earth would he feel deflated by the news that he was not going to be a father? A baby was the last thing he wanted, he reminded himself. 'An unplanned pregnancy would not have been ideal.'

'Not ideal at all.' She sounded brittle. Battered and bruised from her fall down the cliff, she looked infinitely fragile. He recalled her stricken expression when he'd challenged her about the pregnancy test that had fallen out of her bag. Shock had made him react badly.

He guessed she had climbed down the cliff because she'd wanted to hide from him as if he was an ogre. He blenched when he thought that she could have been badly injured or even killed and he would have been to blame. The guilt that had haunted him since he was fourteen reminded him that he destroyed everything good in his life. He wished he could put his arms around Savannah to comfort her and reassure himself that she was unharmed. But she was prickly and defensive.

She went with the nurse to be X-rayed, and an hour later she had been given the all-clear and insisted on walking to the car without help from Dimitris. They were both silent while he drove back to the villa. She spent the journey staring at her phone, and he wondered if it was a tactic to avoid conversation. A chasm had opened up between them and he did not know how to reach her, or if he should try. The truth, he had always known, was that she was safer away from him.

'Go and rest while I make you something to eat,' he told her when he ushered her into the villa. He could not help himself and ran his finger lightly down her pale cheek. A feeling of loss cramped in his gut when she flinched. 'You've had a nasty experience and you are bound to feel the effects of shock, *mátia mou*.'

'Stop.' Her eyes were luminous with tears, but she spoke in a cool voice that chilled him. 'I'm going to my room to pack. I've booked onto a flight to London tonight.'

'Is this because I didn't jump for joy about having a baby?' His jaw clenched. 'What did you expect?'

'I should have expected you to react the way you did,' she said flatly. 'You told me that you can't give me what I want. I guess I hadn't realised until I did the pregnancy test how much I want to have a family one day. These past few weeks that we have spent together were fun, but we both knew our affair had an end date.' She gave him a ghost of a smile. 'We want different things. Nothing has changed from ten years ago. I'm looking for love, the deep, everlasting kind.'

The kind of love that ripped your heart out when it ended abruptly, like when his parents had died. Dimitris didn't want to feel that intensity of pain ever again. He wished he could carry Savannah up to the bedroom they had shared for the past weeks and ignite the passion that always simmered between them. He wanted to show her how good they were together, without love and its associated emotions to create problems. But he couldn't make love to her while she was so fragile and looked achingly vulnerable.

They were compatible physically, and in so many other ways. If only she would see that what they had was enough. *Theós*, he had shared more of himself with her than with any other woman. What more did she want from him? Babies, he thought grimly as he watched her walk slowly up the stairs.

When a taxi pulled up in front of the villa half an hour later, Dimitris stood on his balcony and watched Stefanos carry Savannah's suitcase to the car. He fought the temptation to go after her and beg her not to leave. He was used to his affairs being on his terms. Women did not leave him. Except for Savannah, who had left him twice, a voice in his head taunted him as the taxi drove away.

She'd gone because he wasn't enough for her. She wanted to be loved and it was not an unreasonable request. Her generosity of spirit and boundless compassion meant that she deserved to find love. But she deserved a better man than him. A man who was not afraid to admit his love for her openly and honestly, Dimitris thought bleakly.

# CHAPTER ELEVEN

A MONTH LATER Dimitris acknowledged that he was not looking forward to the party at his publishers. His editorial team and the hierarchy of management were great people, the food was bound to be good, and the champagne would flow. But he did not have any enthusiasm for anything, not the party that would be the first of many during the festive period, nor Christmas, which he would be spending alone this year because Eleni had met a new boyfriend and was going to St Lucia with him. Dimitris had lost his zest for life and only his iron willpower stopped him numbing his pain with a bottle of single malt.

He stood next to the French windows in the drawing room of his house in Richmond. It was ironic that the house was called River Retreat when the river, swollen by the rain that had fallen relentlessly since he'd arrived in London three days ago, had breached the banks and flooded the lawn at the bottom of the garden.

The glorious weather on Australia's Gold Coast had failed to lift his dark mood, and his jaw had ached from forcing himself to smile for the audiences who had packed theatres to watch his cooking demonstrations. At the end of the tour he had returned to Rhodes where the winters were mild. The sun had been shining in the blue sky, but the villa had been full of Savannah, although very much not full of Savannah. Memories of her were everywhere. Her collection of colourful cushions enlivened the neutral décor of the sitting room and her perfume lingered in his bedroom. He often woke in the middle of the night and reached for her, before he remembered that she'd gone.

He had tried to call her to check that there were no repercussions from when she'd fallen down the cliff, but her number had been unavailable. He knew he was fooling himself. What he really wanted to do was beg her to forgive him for behaving so badly when she'd thought she was pregnant and ask her if she could find it in her heart to love him. With a sickening lurch in the pit of his stomach Dimitris knew he was the greatest fool of all time.

He had come to England on a mission. Savannah had confided to him that her relationship with the man she'd believed was her father had been strained, and she'd felt unloved. Dimitris sensed that she was still affected by the rejection she'd experienced as a child. He hoped he could persuade

Savannah's mother to tell her daughter the truth that she deserved to hear.

Savannah had encouraged him to open up about the accident to his sister, and now he was closer to Eleni than ever, and slowly beginning to forgive himself and accept that he could not change the past or predict the future, but a life without love was no life at all. He just hoped he hadn't left the discovery too late to stand a chance with Savannah.

November in England was grey. Grey skies and the dull gleam of rain on grey pavements mirrored Savannah's bleak mood. Christmas was still weeks away, but the shop windows were decorated with festive scenes and the gaudily coloured lights on every high street failed to lift the blanket of misery that had swamped her since she'd left Dimitris.

She couldn't contact him even if she'd wanted to. Somewhere on her journey from Rhodes to London she had lost her phone. It was an old device and because she hadn't backed up her contacts she did not have Dimitris's mobile number. She could probably reach him through his publisher if necessary. But why would she? It was over between them and the sooner she accepted it the better.

By now he would have finished his cooking tour in Australia and had probably returned to Greece, where the weather would be a lot better than in London. Savannah had spent the past weeks looking for somewhere to live and had finally moved into a tiny flat that cost a fortune to rent but was a ten-minute drive away from her mum's nursing home.

She parked her car in front of Willow Grange and ran through the rain to the entrance. She went to her mother's room and found her in bed. Evelyn looked fragile propped against the pillows.

'I'm sorry you had to come out in this awful weather.' To Savannah's consternation, tears filled her mother's eyes.

'Mum—what's wrong?'

'Dimitris came to see me yesterday.'

*Dimitris?* Shock and pain tore through Savannah. She missed him so much. 'What did he want?'

'He asked me to tell you something I should have told you a long time ago. A secret that I have kept from you for far too long.' Evelyn's voice shook. 'I couldn't tell you when Richard was alive because he had sworn me to secrecy. Since he died…well, I should have been honest with you, but I was afraid that you would hate me.'

'Nothing could make me hate you,' Savannah said gently. She could not imagine what secret her mother had kept from her. 'What do you want to tell me?'

'Richard wasn't your father.'

Too shocked to speak, Savannah stared at her mum. From as far back as she could remember, she'd sensed that her father had not loved her. Now finally she understood the reason why she hadn't felt a connection to Richard. She wasn't unlovable, as he had made her feel.

'Then who is my real father?' A memory came to her. 'Was he the man in the photo?'

Evelyn nodded. 'I'll try to explain. I married Richard only a few months after we had met because I was desperate to escape from my bullying stepfather. I was an assistant at an art gallery and Richard liked to boast to people that I worked for Fortescue's. He had come from a poor background and was obsessed with social position.'

She sighed. 'We tried for a baby for five years, but nothing happened. The marriage was strained and I… I fell in love with someone I'd met at the gallery. Johan was a Dutch artist. It was love at first sight for both of us, but I was married. We had a brief affair before Johan returned to Holland and died in a motorbike accident soon after.'

Evelyn wiped her eyes. 'I discovered I was pregnant and confessed to Richard that the baby wasn't his. I was sure he would throw me out. I had fallen out with my family and did not have any money. I was terrified that I would have to give my baby—you—up for adoption.'

'Oh, Mum.' Savannah handed her mother a tissue.

'Richard didn't want a divorce because he thought it would make him look a failure. He agreed to bring you up as his own daughter but made me promise that I would not tell you or anyone the truth. To the outside world we were the perfect family and Richard was a successful businessman. He was determined that you should marry into the aristocracy and encouraged you to accept a proposal from Lord Roxwell's son. But I knew you were not in love with Hugo, and I was glad when you broke off your engagement.'

Savannah's thoughts were reeling. 'You said Dimitris persuaded you to tell me the truth. How did he know that Richard wasn't my father?'

Evelyn shook her head. 'I didn't really understand what he meant. It was something to do with a financial deal that Richard had forced him to accept years ago. Dimitris told me he was worried that your self-confidence had been damaged because Richard hadn't shown you affection when you were growing up. Apparently there was a boyfriend recently who was not honest with you.'

She had nearly let Matt Collier push her into sleeping with him, Savannah remembered. Dimitris was right to guess that she'd felt she had to put up with being treated badly by men because her father—Richard—had made her feel unworthy of being loved. Everything made sense now. At eighteen she'd had a crush on Dimitris even though he hadn't given any indication that he wanted a long-term relationship with her.

Evelyn was tired, and before Savannah left she hugged her mum and assured her that she understood why she'd kept the identity of her real father a secret.

'Richard threatened to stop his financial support for you, including your private school fees,' her mum said tearfully. 'He was manipulative. As the years passed I felt guilty for keeping such a huge secret from you. Dimitris said he felt sure you would be able to forgive me, and you had persuaded him to be honest with his sister.'

When Savannah returned to her car she sat for a few moments, trying to make sense of her whirling thoughts. Her main feeling was of relief that she could let go of her difficult childhood now she knew the truth. She realised that her mum had been in an impossible situation, but she didn't feel so forgiving of Dimitris who, from the sound of it, had been aware for years that Richard was not her father.

On impulse she turned her car towards Richmond. Dimitris had visited her mum the previous day and he might still be in London. The traffic was heavy, and by the time she drove along next to the river the car's engine was making a strange noise. Taking the car to a garage to be serviced was on her list of jobs that she hadn't got round to. Savannah gave a sigh of relief when she saw that the gates in front of River Retreat were open, and a black saloon was parked on the driveway. Dimitris must be here. Her car died just as she turned through the gates. She couldn't change her mind about seeing him now, she thought as she ran through the pouring rain up to the house.

'Savannah?'

She'd expected the housekeeper to open the front door, and her breath left her lungs in a rush when she stared at Dimitris. He looked gorgeous in black jeans and a storm-grey cashmere sweater. Her heart splintered as she studied his sculpted face that looked leaner, so that his cheekbones were sharp and his eyes held a bleakness that shocked her.

The rain had soaked through her sweatshirt and her hair was stuck to her scalp. She shivered, and he immediately opened the door wider. 'Come in. My housekeeper and her husband are in Canada visiting their daughter,' Dimitris explained as he stepped into the cloakroom and returned to hand Savannah a towel. 'You had better take your sweatshirt off, and it can dry in front of the fire.'

Savannah's teeth were chattering, and she felt self-conscious as she pulled her sweatshirt off and gave it to him. She hoped he would think it was the cold that had made her nipples harden so that they jutted through her silk blouse. She followed him into the sitting room, where a log fire was blazing. He waved her to an armchair, but she preferred to stand while she confronted him.

But her temper that had simmered while she'd

driven to his house was replaced with fierce awareness of Dimitris. He rested his arm on the mantelpiece, and she noticed that he'd lost weight. She knew he kept himself fit by working out regularly in the gym, but his whipcord body was leaner, and he looked weary as if he hadn't been sleeping.

'How was Australia?' She felt a sharp stab of jealousy as she imagined him lounging on a beach with a bevy of tanned, toned beauties. Maybe he'd lost weight from a lot of exercise between the sheets.

His dark eyes searched her face. 'I missed you,' he said in an oddly husky voice.

Her heart slammed into her ribs, but she told herself he didn't mean it. After all, he had made no attempt to stop her leaving him in Rhodes. 'I've just been to see Mum. She told me that Richard was not my real father.'

Dimitris exhaled slowly. 'Ah.'

Savannah's anger reignited. 'You *knew.* Why didn't you tell me? Surely I had a right to know?' She frowned as a memory of the previous time she had been at Dimitris's house in Richmond surfaced, and the conversation they'd had over dinner. 'How did you know about the trust fund that my fa... Richard had set up?' she demanded.

'He told me.' Dimitris sighed heavily. 'Richard threatened to prevent you from receiving a fortune that he said was held in trust until you were twenty-five if I did not break off my relationship with you.'

Seeing that Savannah was too shocked to speak, he continued, 'I had initially refused the money he'd offered me as a bribe. But he got nasty and said he wouldn't allow me to screw up his plans for you to marry into a titled family. I called his bluff and told him that I didn't believe he would cause financial harm to his own daughter. That was when he revealed that he wasn't your father. In his words, he had brought up another man's child and paid for your private education, and in repayment he expected you to marry well and increase his social standing.'

Savannah sank down onto the sofa, and Dimitris came and sat down next to her, although he kept a distance from her. 'Richard insisted that I accepted the bribe and never saw you again,' he told her, 'or he would cut off all financial support for you and your mother. You were used to a high standard of living and were about to go to university. I couldn't risk that Richard would carry out his threat.'

'He was a terrible man.' Anger and hurt poured through Savannah as she stared at Dimitris. 'When we met again after ten years you should have told me the truth. Richard was dead by then and couldn't harm Mum or me.'

'It was your mother's secret,' he said tautly. 'I couldn't reveal what I knew.'

She blinked away the tears that filled her eyes. 'I trusted you.' Everything she had believed they'd shared, friends as well as lovers, and a sense that they had grown closer while she had stayed at his villa, had been in her imagination.

Finally Savannah knew that Dimitris would never love her as she deserved to be loved. She had accepted second-best with her brief engagement to Hugo years ago, and with Matt Collier. Neither of them had cared about her. She had hidden her emotions because she'd been afraid of rejection, but there was no shame in loving someone, even if that person would never feel the same way about her.

'I fell in love with you,' she told Dimitris, lifting her chin so she could meet his gaze. 'But you are not the man for me. I want romance, love, a family of my own. I spent a night with you, hoping to free myself of my teenage crush on you. Now I truly am over you.' She stood up and walked over to the door. Her heart was breaking, but next time she would give her heart to a man who appreciated her.

'Savannah…don't go.' Dimitris's voice sounded as if he'd swallowed broken glass.

'There's nothing for me here and no reason to stay.' She was determined to stay strong and fight for the future, the love she wanted, whoever that might be with. She turned to look at him and her lungs felt as if they were being squeezed in a vice when she saw his tortured expression.

Dimitris walked towards her jerkily, with none of

his usual grace. He looked like a man on the edge of hell. 'I love you.'

'Don't,' she whispered. 'Don't joke.'

He put his hands on her shoulders as if he wanted to physically stop her from leaving. His face twisted as if he were in pain when he saw her tears. 'Do you think I would make a joke about the way I feel about you?'

'You don't want a relationship, commitment.' She tried to step away from him, but his fingers tightened and he stared down at her, his eyes blazing with raw emotion that made Savannah's heart thud.

'I want you—*us*,' he told her in a strained voice. 'The weeks we spent together at the villa were the happiest of my life. The only other time I felt that happy was for eleven nights ten years ago, when I held you in my arms and imagined that we were the only two people in the universe and nothing could come between us.'

She shook her head. 'You went away…'

'Richard took a gamble when he told me he wasn't your father. He used emotional blackmail to get me to accept the bribe and never see you again, because he had guessed that I loved you and would do anything to protect your financial security.'

'So you decided it was better for me to have a trust fund rather than for us to be together.' Her voice shook. 'You knew I loved you.'

'Yes, I knew, but I was scared.' Dimitris's jaw

tightened. 'I was afraid to admit to myself how I felt about you. I didn't want to love you because it was agony when my parents were killed. I promised myself that I would never care about anyone so deeply again, so that it couldn't hurt so terribly if I lost that person.'

Savannah felt as though she was standing on the edge of a precipice. She felt dizzy, but she was no longer scared of heights. Dare she believe the fierce emotion blazing in Dimitris's eyes?

He placed his hand under her chin and gently tilted her face up to his. 'I do love you, Savannah. No other woman has ever claimed my heart. It's yours for eternity and I will be committed to you for the rest of my life.'

He cradled her cheek in his palm and wiped away the tears that trickled down her face. 'Don't cry, *agápi mou.*' His jaw clenched. 'You are the sweetest, kindest person and I know you would hate to hurt even me, who once hurt you so badly. If your tears are because you have to tell me that you don't feel the same way about me—' he swallowed '—that you don't love me, then do it quickly.'

She bit her lip. 'I just don't know…' Her words faded and her heart stopped when she saw that Dimitris's eyelashes were wet. And suddenly she did know, and she believed that, impossibly and incredibly, he loved her. It was there in the suspicious brightness in his eyes and the way he swallowed hard. It was there in the faint tremor of his mouth and his hand that shook when he smoothed her hair back from her face so tenderly, so lovingly.

'Oh, Dimitris, I love you too much to ever hurt you. And you love me.' There was wonder in her voice, but certainty too. He loved her and she thought her heart might explode with happiness.

His arms came around her and he pulled her into his heat and strength and held her close to his heart that was thundering in his chest. *S'agapó.* I love you,' he told her over and over again. He kissed her fiercely, and then lifted his head and stared down at her.

'I thought that if I avoided falling in love I would never be hurt. But when you left me I couldn't function, and I realised that denying my love for you was tearing me apart. I knew I had to find you and beg you to give me another chance to prove I can give you everything you want and deserve.'

She held his face in her hands and kissed him with all the love in her heart. 'Prove it now.'

He grinned as he swept her into his arms and carried her upstairs to his bedroom. 'If you insist, *kardiá mou*. I think you are going to be a very bossy wife.'

*'Wife?'*

Dimitris laid her on the bed and tugged the blouse over her head. He cupped her breasts in his palms and let out a ragged breath. '*Theós*, you are beautiful. Will you marry me, Savannah, and make me the happiest man in the world?'

Her smile was pure sunshine. 'I will. Now, will you please stop talking?'

She helped him remove his clothes and he set about rediscovering her body with hands that shook a little and a mouth that worshipped her breasts before he moved lower and pushed her thighs apart. When he entered her it was as if it was the first time, and there was wonder and joy in their lovemaking as they whispered words of love and reached the pinnacle together, before tumbling back down to earth to lie entwined while darkness fell and they were alone in their own private world.

'For ever,' Dimitris vowed. 'Just you and me and the children I hope we will have in the future. He kissed her tenderly. 'The future begins now, my love.'

* * * * *

*Did* Penniless Cinderella for the Greek *blow you away?*
*Then don't miss these other stories by Chantelle Shaw!*

Housekeeper in the Headlines
The Greek Wedding She Never Had
Nine Months to Tame the Tycoon
The Italian's Bargain for His Bride
Her Secret Royal Dilemma

*Available now!*

## #4121 THE MAID MARRIED TO THE BILLIONAIRE

*Cinderella Sisters for Billionaires*

by Lynne Graham

Enigmatic billionaire Enzo discovers Skye frightened and on the run with her tiny siblings. Honorably, Enzo offers them sanctuary and Skye a job. But could their simmering attraction solve another problem—his need for a bride?

## #4122 HIS HOUSEKEEPER'S TWIN BABY CONFESSION

by Abby Green

Housekeeper Carrie wasn't looking for love. Especially with her emotionally guarded boss, Massimo. But when their chemistry ignites on a trip to Buenos Aires, Carrie is left with some shocking news. She's expecting Massimo's twins!

## #4123 IMPOSSIBLE HEIR FOR THE KING

*Innocent Royal Runaways*

by Natalie Anderson

Unwilling to inflict the crown on anyone else, King Niko didn't want a wife. But then he learns of a medical mix-up. Maia, a woman he's never met, is carrying his child! And there's only one way to legitimize his heir...

## #4124 A RING TO CLAIM HER CROWN

by Amanda Cinelli

To become queen, Princess Minerva must marry. So when she sees her ex-fiancé, Liro, among her suitors, she's shocked! The past is raw between them, but the more time she spends in Liro's alluring presence, the more wearing anyone else's ring feels unthinkable...

## #4125 THE BILLIONAIRE'S ACCIDENTAL LEGACY

*From Destitute to Diamonds*

by Millie Adams

When playboy billionaire Ewan "loses" his Scottish estate to poker pro Jessie, he doesn't expect the sizzling night they end up sharing… So months later when he sees a photo of a very beautiful, very *pregnant* Jessie, a new endgame is required. He's playing for keeps!

## #4126 AWAKENED ON HER ROYAL WEDDING NIGHT

by Dani Collins

Prince Felipe must wed promptly or lose his crown. And though model Claudine is surprised by his proposal, she agrees. She's never felt the kind of searing heat that flashes between them before. But can she enjoy the benefits of their marital bed without catching feelings for her new husband?

## #4127 UNVEILED AS THE ITALIAN'S BRIDE

by Cathy Williams

Dante needs a wife—urgently! And the business magnate looks to the one woman he trusts…his daughter's nanny! It's just a mutually beneficial business arrangement. Until their first kiss after "I do" lifts the veil on an inconvenient, inescapable attraction!

## #4128 THE BOSS'S FORBIDDEN ASSISTANT

by Clare Connelly

Brazilian billionaire Salvador retreated to his private island after experiencing a tragic loss, vowing not to love again. When he's forced to hire a temporary assistant, he's convinced Harper Lawson won't meet his scrupulous standards… Instead, she exceeds them. If only he wasn't drawn to their untamable forbidden chemistry…

---